THE DEMON TAILOR

SUSAN MCCAULEY

CELTIC SEA PUBLISHING

CONTENTS

PREFACE

The following tale is based on the real-life sixteenth-century French serial killer and self-proclaimed lycanthrope known as the Demon Tailor. He was burned at the stake for his crimes in December 1598.

CHAPTER 1

I was seventeen years old when the demon tailor captured me.

Of course, he did not go by that name when he carried me away from my home. And his true name has now been erased from all of history. *Damnatio Memoriae.* His memory damned for all eternity. Except I know it. I know his name. I cannot scour him from my mind or my flesh no matter how hard I've tried these past six months.

So I shall tell my story here in hopes of freeing myself from him and the terrible things he did. And, perhaps, it will shine a light on his torturous crimes. Not to glorify or to remember him. No. But so the villagers and citizens will know what to look for should the likes of him ever walk the earth again. Yet I pray with all fervor that will never happen.

His name was Jacques Albinet. He captured me in the woods outside our home on the outskirts of Paris in November 1598.

I awoke earlier than usual, before the rooster crowed to welcome the sun. I swung my legs over the edge of my paillasse, a straw-stuffed pallet covered in scratchy canvas, set upon a little wooden frame, and picked a juicy flea from my thigh, crushing it between my fingers. My bare feet touched the rough plank flooring of the second-story room I shared with my little sister, Collette. *Mon chou.* My sweetie. Her wavy chestnut hair twisted over her face, Collette was still curled in sleep, her small fingers clutching the doll I made for her when our brother, Pierre, had gone missing.

My heart twisted painfully in my chest, but I shoved away the unwanted feeling. Today I would not miss Pierre. Today I would not have to work at the inn we called home. It was more than a home, really; it was our livelihood. Papa and Mère, my little sister and brother and me. We lived here and worked in Le Poulet Fou. Well, until my brother, Pierre, disappeared in October. But, no, I chided myself. I would not think on Pierre today. Today Papa was taking me with him to the heart of Paris!

I slipped quietly out of bed so as not to wake Collette and pulled my second-best kirtle over my chemise. I had only one nice dress and two for work at the inn. I snugged the laces at the front of my kirtle and pinned my sleeves, then slipped on my shoes and scampered down to the kitchen.

Mère was already at work, her skilled hands swiftly chopping cabbage and potherbs for the evening pottage. A stack of hard biscuits was neatly placed on a platter beside her. We must be out of grain. Likely Papa and I would buy millet, oats, and rye, and also a few day-old loaves at the market in Les Halles. My mouth watered at the thought of tasting wheat bread still warm from the oven. It was a rare treat on market day, and one Mère would forbid if I asked for permission. So I would smile sweetly at Papa, and he would buy me some nice, fresh bread. *Peuh* to Mère! She could eat the hard rye biscuits on her own. Papa and I would enjoy our freshly baked wheat bread in secret —together.

At the market, I knew we would visit the vintner for wine and one of the many food stalls to buy salted pork and fish for our pottage as well as cheese. And I would get to see the latest fashions and the wealthy ladies all dressed in their silk skirts with full sleeves and lavish collars. Their hair would be decorated with pearls and jewels . . . while I still wore a linen coif.

Yet we would not tarry long for me to gape. We must do the shopping and return to Le Poulet Fou before nightfall to avoid the dangers of robbers who too often lurked in the darkened alleyways of Paris and beside the roads outside the city, and to help Mère with our evening guests at the inn. It would be a long but exciting day.

"Good morning, Mère." I was so excited about going to Les Halles that I pecked a rare kiss on her pale, icy cheek, but she hardly smiled. That was so like Mère. Always working, never smiling. Unless it was a smile to a paying customer. She was generous with smiles if money was involved. She had never smiled much at our family, but I do remember she would sing to me when I was small. *Ma petite fille* she would call me. Her little girl. Then she'd sing "Le Carillon de Vendôme" as I drifted to sleep.

She'd stopped singing when Pierre was a little boy, and I'd been left to sing to him and Collette. I didn't know what made Mère so unhappy. So unfeeling. Mère had not cried when Pierre disappeared. He was fifteen and near enough to manhood, she'd said. She said he'd likely run off with his girl Nicole from down the lane. But it wasn't like Pierre to disappear without a word. He would have told me, I'm certain of it. Yet she didn't seem to care.

It was Papa who had looked down the road as the sun set on the second evening—and every evening thereafter—with tears in his eyes, silently praying for Pierre's return. I scolded myself for thinking about such things and reminded myself I would not grieve Pierre today.

"Good morning, Marie," Mère said, tossing the chopped cabbage into the cauldron. "Be certain to see the vintner today." She wiped her hands on her linen apron, crossed to the money box that she and Papa kept hidden beneath a loose board in the kitchen floor, and brought me a small sack of coins. "Take this. Buy three loaves of day-old bread and some grain—rye and barley and millet, but not too much wheat. We cannot afford much wheat. And do not forget the salt barrel herring."

How could I forget the herring! Sometimes it seemed our days of eating tough, salted fish might never end. The Church prohibited eating meat for nearly a third of the year, and so we ate fish. *Peuh!* I would be happy if I never saw another salted herring again. And even happier to leave my life at Le Poulet Fou for the arms of a wealthy merchant. Ha! Mère would slap me if I were to say that aloud. She would likely send me to Father François *before* Sunday Mass to plead for forgiveness. At least there would be no fish today. Mère was busy making our usual pottage of salted bacon and cabbage.

"Yes, Mère." I bobbed my head politely, as if she were a stranger in charge of a shop—since Pierre had gone missing, I felt not much closer to her than that. How could I when she did not mourn the loss of my brother?

After breaking my fast with a hard biscuit and a dab of preserved summer berries, I stepped into the yard to look in on Papa. His balding head greeted me like a pale moon as he stooped over our chestnut mare, Symonne, preparing her and our two-wheeled cart to go into the city. The cart was a spindly, light thing, but sturdy enough for Symonne to pull us and our provisions back from Paris.

"Good morning, Papa." I smiled, then patted Symonne's shiny neck. "Good morning, Symonne." I kissed her soft muzzle She snorted at me in reply and nuzzled my face with her wet nose.

"Good morning, *ma petite fille*." His little girl. When we were alone, Papa still called me that. Papa smiled at me as he placed the bridle on Symonne, readying her for our journey. It would take a good part of the morning to get into the city and a bit longer still to make our way through the crowded streets and into Les Halles.

The autumn sun shined brightly across my face, making my russet hair glow golden red. The air held the crisp promise of autumn and a hint of excitement. We turned up a muddy, rutted road heading north toward the Seine. If only Pont Neuf was complete! We could then make our journey across the river to Les Halles with more haste. Alas, it was still being put in place—stone by stone—one archway at a time. And so strange it was to see a bridge with no houses being built upon it! Mayhap our Good King Henry would change his mind once the bridge was complete. God knew the city needed more places to house its inhabitants.

We traveled farther east, Symonne clopping through the muddy roads, past the other citizens heading to buy or sell or trade at the market, and finally, we turned onto the

Pont Notre-Dame. Wooden houses rose up on either side of us, some as high as five stories. There was a bustle of activity—some women sang, some hung out laundry to dry, others tossed their night waste into the street where it ran in reeking, muddy troughs down the center of the road. I wrinkled my nose at the stench. I suppose there was no place for a cesspool if you had a house on the bridge— one could simply toss it into the river. Still, the stench of human waste made my nose burn and my eyes water. I gagged, thankful—for a brief moment—to live outside the city. *Beurk!* Still, if I married a wealthy merchant, I would gladly trade in my life at Le Poulet Fou for a home in Paris. Ah, Paris! All the sights and sounds and fashions. I would visit Mère and Papa and Collette at the inn, but what a life I could have in the city.

Papa spoke little on our journey, and I feared his heart was heavy with thoughts of Pierre. Pierre who, until a fortnight past, used to travel with him into the city on market days instead of me. Pierre his only son. I wondered if Papa was silent while we rode because he was looking for Pierre —searching each face in the crowded streets for one he so longed to see—or merely praying to God for my brother's return.

I shook the longing from my mind and let the *clip-clop* of Symonne's hooves against the road lull me into a state of bliss. I enjoyed sitting. It was rare to sit and have a rest at Le Poulet Fou. Making meals and serving guests and cleaning took most of my time at home, but now I sat and watched. I watched as men and women scurried past us, their cloaks and tunics covered in road dust. I watched dirty children dash in and out of the road playing blind man's bluff, barely dodging piles of horse dung and the wheels of carts that passed hazardously close to them.

Finally, we saw the tower of Saint-Jacques-de-la-

Boucherie rise above us. The Church of Saint-Jacques was crafted of rich white stone with prickly spires and a colorful stained-glass wheel, blues and reds and greens and oranges sparkling in the sun. As the church was dedicated to the butchers of the city, I knew we were close to the market, and my heart soared.

We soon turned along a lane that ran beside the Holy Innocents' Church, and a repugnant smell even worse than that of piss struck me like a blow to the face. We were approaching Holy Innocents' Cemetery. "Cover your nose and mouth, Marie. The wind is not in our favor this day."

I did as Papa bade me. "Why does it smell so foul, Papa?" I asked, my face hidden beneath the collar of my chemise. The few times I'd been past this spot before, the odor had not been so vile.

"There are too many bodies and not enough space, *ma petite fille*. They have not enough room to bury the dead. Some are mounds of corpse wax when they are moved to the charnel houses to make room for more bodies." He shook his head as if weighing the problem.

I'd heard of the overflowing corpses in Holy Innocents' Cemetery, but I didn't know of the wretched odor and had never considered such a problem as where to bury the dead. And to think the cemetery was right beside Les Halles! Who would want to buy meat and cheese with the stench of rotting corpses wafting across their noses? *Beurk!* I coughed and kept my nose and mouth tucked beneath the collar of my chemise.

Papa stopped our cart and tied Symonne to a tethering ring where others had tied their mounts for market day. With a hand from Papa, I climbed out of the cart, careful not to let my kirtle drag in a large pile of horse dung I had to hop over to avoid.

7

"Right, we must buy barley and rye," Papa said, reviewing Mère's list aloud.

"But not too much wheat." I tried to keep the hint of mockery from my voice.

Papa's eyes scolded me, but then he smiled. "No. Not too much wheat. But you know I always bring a little extra for our treat." He held up a coin and placed it in my hand. "Today we shall have *pain bourgeois*. A fine little loaf of wheat bread."

I leapt up and kissed Papa on both cheeks. "I love you, Papa." And I did love him. He brought joy to my life, whereas Mère brought sternness and work. Yet I should not be so harsh to Mère. She loved us in her own way. Mère had been raised by a strict mother who had served in the house of a wealthy lord in Paris. As a girl, Mère had become best of friends with the lord's daughter, Marie, the girl from whom I took my name. Marie had not wanted to be separated from Mère, so Mère and Marie would take lessons together with the girl's tutors. It was there Mère had learned to read and write and do arithmetic. She would probably still be with Marie had she not fallen in love with Papa. But all of her learning had come in use for running our inn. And she had made certain to teach Papa and her children everything she knew about reading and writing and sums.

Papa rattled off the rest of our list. "Sausage, bacon, spices, and . . ."

"A barrel of salted herring," we sang together, ending with a laugh. With one hundred days of fasting each year, we could never have too much salted herring on hand for ourselves or our guests. The one time Papa and Pierre had not returned with a barrel of fish, Mère had threatened to make them sleep in the stable with Symonne all night. Ha!

They had returned immediately to the market for the herring.

Les Halles was overflowing with people. Elbow to elbow we pushed our way through the masses gawping at and arguing with merchants over the goods and food for sale. There were stalls with chandlers and spoon sellers, and others with plates and bowls on display. Then there was the food! So many butchers and bakers and spice sellers. The fragrances of cinnamon, ginger, and cardamom nearly overpowered the stench of rotting corpses from the cemetery across the road. Soon the smell of rot had almost disappeared completely.

Papa first stopped at a smeremongere's stall where a man, his wife, and their young son had tallow candles on display along with vinegar, cheese, and soap. I sniffed a lovely bar of lavender soap while Papa haggled with the smeremongere for a bundle of candles, a round of Gruyére, and a large slab of cheddar. Once a price was agreed upon and our debt settled, we moved from the smeremongere's stall to an area overtaken by butchers. My eyes bulged with visions of salted sides of pork, sausage, and bacon. There was also mutton and poultry and some types of game I could not fathom a guess. Fresh and salted fish was also for sale. After buying sausage, a side of salted pork, and *two* barrels of salted herring, we went to the spice stalls.

Oh, how I loved the spices! There was black pepper and golden saffron, reddish cinnamon and copper-colored cloves. The smells made my mouth water with thoughts of Christmas pudding. Papa bought some ginger, black pepper, and a small measure of salt. But my favorite stalls were the bakers with their delicious bread and pretty little cakes and cookies and tarts for sale. I'd once shared a sweet ginger cake with Pierre and Collette on my name day. It was the most deliciously wonderful thing I'd ever tasted. Today the baker had mince pies, gingerbread cookies in the shape of deer and birds, and bread. Fresh, hot bread. A well-dressed woman with a pinched nose and bird-like mouth, likely the servant of a lord or lady, stood before us purchasing *pain de chapitre*. The baker's finest tarts and cakes. She purchased so many that her basket bulged and I thought there would be nothing left for us!

Finally, she finished her order. Papa rewarded me for my patience when he bought us *pain bourgeois* with the coin he had given me. 'Twas a pretty little loaf, crusty on the outside and buttery soft and warm inside. I gave half to Papa, and took a dainty bite from my portion. It nearly melted in my mouth, and my eyes must have rolled in my head. Bite by savory bite, I ate it where we stood until there was nothing left but the warm memory on my fingertips.

With my heart and belly full, I took Papa's hand and he led me toward our cart to go home. That's when we heard a loud, passionate voice calling out above the heads of the crowd. "Listen! Everyone come closer and listen! There is another wolf among us! A beast that hunts and kills our women and children. Join me in hunting him down to protect our families and our homes!"

I stopped in the trodden road and looked to Papa, fear lacing my voice. "A wolf?" I swallowed a marble of fear beginning to make its way into my throat. "You and Pierre saw a werewolf trial only six months ago. Could there be another? So soon?"

Papa clutched our market goods beneath his arm, squeezed my hand in his other, and smiled a smile that didn't quite reach his eyes. "Look and listen, Marie. And we shall find out."

The man who spoke with such fervor stood atop a small wooden platform to address the crowd. He was young, likely not more than twenty. His muscular arms made me think he might be a blacksmith, or a journeyman at least. His handsome face was alight with concern, and his blue eyes flashed around the crowd. His gaze snagged on me, and I felt myself blush, glad Papa was focused on him and not me. Glad Papa could not read the thoughts that made me feel warm and tingly.

"A black hooded figure has been seen in the woods. Cattle have been killed. Our children are missing!" He looked at me again, his blue eyes aflame with passion. "Our brothers and sisters—taken from us in the night. We must attempt to find them and stop the monster who hunts them down."

My blush faded, and my cheeks turned cold. *Oh, God, no.* It could not be that Pierre was one of the children taken by such a monster. I would not even let myself think it.

"Bring your weapons. Bring your tools. Bring anything you can to hunt the beast. We need men and boys strong enough to fight!"

Urgent mumbles of anger and fear spread through the crowd like wildfire, but no one stepped forward.

"We'll meet tonight and seek him out in the woods where he was last seen—just south of Pont Neuf."

"Papa, that's near the inn," I whispered.

"Shhh, Marie. Look and listen, don't speak." Papa's gaze was fixed upon the man, his brow furrowed in concern.

"Who will come with me to hunt the beast?" His gaze swept the large crowd, eyes narrowed that no hands were raised. Not a single person stepped forward. They merely stirred, angry and uneasy, but were too afraid to move.

I did not want to see the handsome young man falter in his plea and risk a beast being loose in the woods hunting down boys like Pierre. Without thinking, I stepped forward. Losing control of my lips, I called out over the crowd, "I will hunt with you."

"Marie!" Papa hissed, cringing at my brash words.

The crowd laughed, but none more loudly than the handsome young man seeking help. "You?" He leapt down from the overturned cask upon which he stood. "You're a pretty little thing. There's no place for the likes of you on a hunt in the woods with a bunch of burly, sweaty men and cheeky boys!"

My cheeks flushed again, but I tilted my chin up. I was pleased he'd called me pretty, but infuriated that he thought I had no place in the woods. "I'm as capable as any man!" I said, fiercely meeting his gaze. And I loved the woods by Le Poulet Fou. I *knew* them—certainly better than him.

The young man looked me up and down, then with a chortle turned to Papa. "Take your daughter home, sir. It is the likes of her who have been taken by the monster we hunt."

Papa inclined his head, resigned to my outburst, but friendly as always. "I'm Antoine Laudin, *monsieur*, and this is my daughter Marie."

"Marie." The young man took my hand and kissed it. I fought to stay angry with this handsome stranger who'd just embarrassed me, but now let his lips linger on my hand.

"I am Tristan de Marchey, at your service." He smiled, his clear blue eyes never leaving mine.

Papa cleared his throat. "We live at the inn, Le Poulet Fou, near the woods you speak of. You and your—hunters —can meet there if you like. And I will keep my daughter safely indoors." Papa firmly gripped my hand as if I were a child being scolded. The young man's eyes sparkled with mirth. Right then I hated Papa and his embarrassing words. I wished I could crawl into our cart and disappear forever. *Peuh!* to them both.

"Thank you, sir," he said, dismissing me with a smirk and a turn of his shoulders. Then he addressed the crowd. "For those of you as brave as this girl, we will meet tonight at Le Poulet Fou, the inn just south of Pont Neuf. Come armed."

CHAPTER 2

A blackened log snapped in the hearth fire, shooting orange embers upward into the smoky room and taking the nip out of the chill autumn air. It was my favorite time of year. Cool, but not cold. Fresh and crisp, so my shawl barely kept the gooseflesh from prickling up along my arms and back when I was in the garden collecting vegetables or herbs for our daily pottage.

In the daytime, my eyes would feast on the orange and yellow leaves, crunchy and rustling amongst the branches of the woods just beyond our home. Pierre would've helped me in the yard. Together we would've fed the chickens and sheep. We would've tended the garden, picked the season's vegetables, and talked about our hopes and dreams. Oh, how I missed Pierre.

Papa thought Pierre left to find an apprenticeship in the heart of Paris. Mère said he fell in love and ran away to be with Nicole, the girl who lived down the lane. She disappeared not long after my brother. But I think the wolves took them. Papa and Mère laughed at me and told me that wolves don't take children. They said such stories are made up to keep children out of the woods at night and away from strangers, and that I'm too old to believe in such things.

I said *peuh!* They should not have sent Pierre through the woods—alone—to the vintner to bring back more wine for our guests. No. They should have sold our cider and had Papa go with Pierre during the day to buy more wine. But no. They had to have it. They didn't want to lose money for their precious inn, so instead they lost their only son. And I lost my brother.

That's the problem with living at an inn. Papa and Mère care more about their customers than their own children. At least Mère does, and Papa does what he must to keep her happy. There's never any rest. People are always here. Always talking and laughing and drinking and fighting. Mostly people from our part of the city come, but sometimes there are travelers. They come to eat and drink and forget their troubles. And yet they cause me many— the rowdy, cup-shotten men with their roving eyes and wandering hands traveling to places they should not go. I bat them away with a coy smile—enough to put them in their place, but not enough to keep them from coming back for more wine and cider and ale. Mère has made sure I know how to protect my virtue while keeping the customers happy. And I had my regulars—all of whom were here tonight.

There was Iean, the hairy brute who slurred when he was drunk and tried to grab my tail, or that of any maiden who passed him. There was Hubert, the skinny fellow with gaping yellow teeth whose hosiery never stayed put, but always sagged beneath his bony knees. And then there was Charles. Sweet, kindly Charles with his sparkling brown eyes and handsomely crooked smile. He was nice to gaze upon and looked at me like a puppy. But he wanted less in life than I. He smiled at me now, eagerly beckoning me forward before Monsieur Couture began his tales for the evening entertainment.

"Good evening, Charles." I smiled and poured ale into his mug. "Anything for supper this night?"

"Pottage and bread, if you have it." He gazed up at me with the same longing I'd seen in his eyes for the past two seasons.

I nodded and went to fetch his supper, but he gently grabbed my hand. "Have you spoken with your papa yet, Marie? About what I said? About what we discussed?"

I pulled away from his work-hardened hands. "Not yet."

His eyes implored me. "Marie, please speak to your papa. I'm certain he will let us marry, and I can lighten his load at the inn. Then, one day, when your mère and papa are old and feeble, we can care for them and run the inn. Just think, Marie, we could have a family of our own and raise them here at Le Poulet Fou!"

"Perhaps." I smiled sweetly. *If only you were a Parisian merchant or shopkeeper, Charles, then I would marry you.* But I would much rather leave Le Poulet Fou and make a home in the heart of Paris—not stay here to serve these cup-shotten fools. Perhaps then I'd have a child or two. I would teach them their letters and numbers, and we could run a shop together. But I would not make them work from morning 'til dark serving wine and cider and food and scrubbing floors and pewter cups and plates as I did each day. And that is what Charles dreamt of—to stay here at Le Poulet Fou. *Beurk!* That was his dream, not mine.

Ah, well. I had little time to dwell on such things. Charles's request would continue to wait until I found my true love, or I grew too old to put him off any longer. For now, there were meals to serve and drinks to fill.

I turned to pour a tankard of cider, but stopped when

the door of the inn burst open. My heart fluttered beneath my ribs. The young man, Tristan, who'd been seeking wolf hunters in Paris, led a group of about a dozen men and boys inside. It was a befouled-looking group. Some were mere boys; others were men with their clothes unkempt or dirty, likely come from a hard day in the trades. Most were armed with pitchforks and butcher knives.

With confidence that made my heart pound and my cheeks flush, Tristan leapt upon the only empty table and stomped his foot until all conversation ceased. "We've come to hunt the monster in the woods, be it man or wolf. Join us if you will, and I guarantee an ale and a meal to the man who captures or kills the beast!"

A cheer rang out from within the inn, but none so much as from the bedraggled band Tristan had brought with him. No doubt some of the boys were street urchins hoping for a free meal.

Charles grabbed my arm and pulled me close. "Another wolf, Marie? Have you seen anything in the woods?" His kind, earnest eyes searched my face. "Could that be what happened to Pierre?"

"I don't know, but I've seen nothing out of the ordinary in the woods. I think these men are merely hungry for adventure."

Charles's grip remained tight on my wrist. "Don't go out there any longer. Not alone. Not at night."

I scoffed. "If I wait for Mère or Papa to come with me, then our herb stores will run dry as will our vegetables. No. I will do as I must."

"Marie!" Alarm lit his voice, and he stared hard into my eyes.

"But," I sighed. "I shall not wander too far from the house, and I will try not to go out at night."

Looking only somewhat mollified, Charles loosened his

grip on my wrist so I could pull away. "Just please be careful."

I nodded, then turned away from Charles to serve our patrons. I came face-to-face with Tristan's excited, alluring eyes.

"Ah, hello, Marie." He smiled and kissed my hand as if he were a gentleman. "Have you reconsidered your offer to go traipsing off in the woods with me tonight to seek out the beast?"

Charles stiffened behind me, and I smiled boldly into Tristan's arrogant gaze. "I have thought on it, yes. And I still think I'm just as capable as any man at hunting a beast."

Tristan snorted with laughter and put his arm around me in a too familiar fashion that made Charles leap to his feet, knocking over his chair. At this, Tristan squeezed me closer so I could smell the sweat and woods and excitement on him. "*Ma chérie*, I want nothing to happen to you," he whispered in a way that gave me shivers, then kissed me on the head. "So stay inside tonight with your mère and let the men keep you safe."

Arrogant fool, I thought. Angry with myself for being thrilled with his whispered words and enjoying the warmth of his body pressing against mine.

Charles stepped beside me, so close that Tristan took a step back, releasing me from his embrace. "You have no need to worry for her safety, I assure you. I will look after Marie."

Tristan weighed Charles with his eyes. "We shall both look after her, *monsieur*. Then she'll be that much safer." Tristan gave me a flirtatious smile, which made Charles's clenched fist bump into my arm. "I'll see you after the hunt, *ma chérie*. You can share a meal with me."

Of course Charles decided to go with the men to hunt the beast. Why would he not? *Peuh!* Foolish boy. Foolish men, the lot of them! Out hunting a beast in the woods at night. Why not wait until the light? They said 'twas because the beast hunted only at night and slept in his hidden lair during the day. I thought they merely wanted to have stories to tell the women and their children over ale and wine. Stories to make them sound brave.

Still, I hoped Charles would be safe and not do something stupid because of Tristan and his boastful words. I could just imagine sweet Charles getting himself into a fight with the likes of Tristan. He wouldn't survive such a contest. And I wouldn't put up with Tristan's arrogant remarks. Women were just as able as men, whether Tristan knew it or not. No. I would sneak into the woods tonight and help the men hunt for the beast, and in so doing, I would also keep watch over Charles.

I discarded my apron and grabbed my worn scarlet cloak, which I fastened securely around my neck and shoulders. It was old, something Mère used to wear before she'd made a new one, but still, it was warm and it was mine, and it wouldn't do at all for me to catch a chill. I considered grabbing a knife or some other means of protection, but Mère might see me. Besides, if I lost track of the men, I would not be able to be part of their adventure.

After the din of the men's raucous laughter died to a murmur, I grabbed the only object nearby, a thick wooden spoon, and crept out through the small door in the kitchen that led to the garden and the woods beyond. The sun had already set behind the trees, and the faint seam of orange that lit the horizon faded before my eyes. I followed the sound of the men's voices to the edge of the woods where I could hear Tristan clearly.

"We'll split into groups of four, each taking a different direction." Through the flickering torchlight, I could see the outline of Tristan's arm as he motioned to different parts of the woods. "We need to spread out to cover more ground, but stay close enough that we can call for help if we find the beast." A murmur of assent arose from the small crowd, and just as quickly, with their torches and axes and heads held high, they disappeared into the woods.

If I was going to venture into this folly—and it did seem a folly to me now that I stood in the chill night air beneath the full moon—it was time for me to follow. What would I do if I found the beast? A kitchen spoon did not make much of a weapon, lest I beat the creature over the head to defend myself. The beast would likely snap it in two. Would I scream like a terrified girl? I sighed. Mayhap Tristan had been right and I should be in the inn with my mère. I shivered. No. I would not be bested by an arrogant man. I was not afraid, and I would not stay back with the women and children and elderly. I would go into the woods and search for the beast. Then I would call for help, and together we would capture or kill the monster if we found it.

I shook off the chill of fear that coursed through me as goose bumps rippled over my flesh. I scanned the groups until I found the one I wanted—the one with the stocky form of Charles lingering at its edge. He was the only man holding a rake. Had I not been worried for him, I would have laughed. He looked like a farmer, not a warrior. Did he actually think he could fight off a werewolf, let alone a regular wolf or even an angry man, with a mere rake? At least those with axes could sever the beast's head. Still, I chided myself, a rake was better than a spoon, which is what I had, but if I turned back now to get a real weapon, I would surely lose them in the darkened tangle of branches that lay ahead.

Hunched low, I crept through the garden, careful not to twist my ankle in a hole from which I'd recently plucked turnips. The soft, loose dirt crumbled beneath my feet, sneaking its way into my goatskin shoes and clinging between my toes. Through the low light of the deepening night, I kept my eyes on Charles. He was in the group farthest to my left, for which I was thankful. That meant no one from another group would bump into me. So I veered wide. Staying to the left of Charles's group, I emerged from the safety of the garden and crept into the darkness of the woods. The scents of the forest at night enveloped me: loam and pine and the nip of juniper. And the sounds. Rustling branches. The haunting *hoo* of the eagle-owl. The echo of the men's footsteps upon the bracken and fallen branches. Their muffled whispers, louder than they intended, echoing through the gloom.

I hadn't realized how dark the woods would be at night, and of course I hadn't thought to bring a torch. Even if I had, I wouldn't have done so. A torch would give me away to the men. Or the beast. Blinded by darkness, I stumbled forward. Branches crunched and twisted beneath my feet, clawing at my legs and twisting in my skirt. Sweat beaded on my forehead and streamed into my eyes as I trudged through the tangled underbrush, trying to keep up with Charles's faint outline. Finally, when I could neither hear nor see any of the men, I stopped and looked around —the woods I thought I knew so well had become foreign. I saw no flickering torches or movement. I strained my ears, listening for the sound of voices or footsteps. Silence, save for the odd rustle of the wind caressing the leaves.

A branch broke to my right. Not a simple twig, but

something large that cracked with a groaning snap beneath the foot or claw of something large. I froze, my breath catching in my throat. My heart hammered into my ribs, and I tried not to utter a sound. Was it one of the men from the hunting party? Or was it something worse?

Staring hard into the space where I'd heard the sound, I saw movement. I could scarcely make out the black figure in the darkness. It couldn't be Charles unless he had come up from behind me, and I knew his group was up ahead. I stared harder, trying to discern the shape. It looked to be a large man in a dark hooded cape, creating an even darker void in the night. Then the figure stopped. The shape of a cowled head rose so that the hidden face beneath was looking directly at me.

That's when I saw its eyes—two gleaming, bloody red orbs piercing me through the darkness. With a shriek of fright, I dropped my spoon amongst the brambles, tripped over a broken log, and scrambled backward. I clambered to my knees, dirt and moss wedging itself beneath my nails as I struggled to stand.

Suddenly a hand clamped over my mouth. Searing heat shot through my veins, and my neck burned as I twisted my head to find my attacker.

"Shhh, Marie. It's me. It's Charles." He held me at arm's length, looking into my eyes, trying to calm me. "You're safe."

With a sob of relief, I slapped at his chest, then fell into him, relieved and angry at my screech of fright. "How did you find me?" I asked, my voice breathless, ragged. I'd been so sure I had ventured into the woods unseen.

"I caught a movement at the edge of the garden. I wasn't sure, but I stayed at the outside of my group to look for you." He shook his head at my foolishness, but the kindness never left his eyes. "It won't do for your papa to catch you out here . . . or any of the others. That Tristan would make a right scene."

I scowled and pulled away from him, but not so far that I left the safety of his torchlight.

"Have you found anything, Charles?" a voice called through the darkened branches.

He held the torch toward the voice, leaving me in a pool of darkness. "Nothing. I'm going to head back to the inn soon—before we've gone too far into unknown territory. We should look for its lair when it is light."

"You're right. We should go back," came the voice, quivering with nervousness.

"Go on with the others. I can find my way back from here," Charles called. He looked at me, his eyes telling me to keep quiet. I didn't want to obey, but I knew he was right. Papa would ban me from going to Paris, or anyplace outside the inn, if he learned I'd snuck out after the men. Especially since Pierre had gone missing.

"We'll see you back at the inn," another deep voice called, and their footsteps retreated, fading away as they trod upon the underbrush.

"Come then." Charles extended a hand to me, safe and warm. "We'll return together. And if they ask questions, I'll tell them we were checking the perimeter of the inn and garden to make sure everything was secure." I was thankful for the gesture. Thankful Charles was willing to lie to protect me. Thankful it was Charles who'd found me in the woods and not some man or monster.

I took his hand, hoping he didn't take my gesture as a promise of affection. I would accompany him back to the inn and let him make excuses to Mère and Papa about why I had been outside. If they even noticed to ask.

CHAPTER 3

*M*ère was busy in the kitchen, and Papa was serving supper when I returned. Papa spared me a questioning glance but nothing more as the small crowd of men and boys settled in from their fruitless hunt, filling the inn to bursting. Mère was delighted; she flitted about filling glasses and giggling in a very un-Mère way. The more patrons we had, the better Mère's mood.

The wine flowed, and so did the stories. And that night the stories would be especially grand, for we had the great Monsieur Couture telling of "Le Petit Chaperon Rouge." At least he was someone I liked. And I looked forward to his tales—even if they frightened me.

Monsieur Couture raised his large, hairy fist and made as if to pound on an imaginary door. His usually deep voice forced up a notch as if he were Little Red Riding Hood herself. "'Hello, Grand-mère. It is your grandchild who has brought you a cake and a little pot of butter Mother sends you.'"

Looking around the room with hungry eyes, Monsieur Couture dropped his voice into an extra deep, booming tenor of a beast with the crackling edge of an old woman's voice. "'Pull the bobbin, and the latch will go up.'" Then he continued in his usual baritone, "So Little Red Riding Hood pulled the bobbin, and the door opened. The wolf—the great *lupum*—seeing her come in, said to her, hiding himself under the bedclothes, 'Put the cake and the little pot of butter upon the stool, and come get into bed with me.'"

Monsieur Couture looked around the inn. Once satisfied all eyes were on him, he continued his tale. "So Little Red Riding Hood took off her clothes and got into bed. She was greatly amazed to see how her grandmother looked in her nightclothes and said to her, 'Grand-mère, what big arms you have!'"

I delivered Charles's supper with an extra smile; he had truly saved me from being embarrassed in front of Tristan and the men and from being scolded by Mère and Papa. If only he wanted more than a mere life at the inn. I sighed, then filled a patron's mug with hard cider, and paused to listen to the story. Everyone was enraptured. Even the old men who'd been bent over their dice game now looked up to listen.

"'All the better to hug you with, my dear,'" boomed Monsieur Couture.

"'Grand-mère, what big legs you have!'" His voice flipped up a notch to that of him pretending to be a little girl. Monsieur Couture's voice carried up and down, like wind rippling through the trees as he answered himself.

"'All the better to run with, my child.'

"'Grand-mère, what big ears you have!'

"'All the better to hear with, my child.'

"'Grand-mère, what big eyes you have!'

"'All the better to see with, my child.'

"'Grand-mère, what big teeth you have!'

"'All the better to eat you up with!'" Monsieur Couture

leaned forward and snarled at the entranced listeners. "And saying these words, this wicked *lupum* fell upon Little Red Riding Hood and ate her all up."

His eyes floated from me to the small figure lingering in the doorway to our living quarters. "Mind my words, Collette," said Monsieur Couture, looking at my wide-eyed little sister. "Don't go out alone at night. Especially not into the woods. And never—ever—talk to strangers!" And with a growl, Monsieur Couture took a last, long swig of his wine, and a burst of applause erupted from the tables around him.

I hurried over to Collette, her face pale and terrified. "Oh, *mon chou*. What are you doing here? You should be preparing for bed, not listening to the monsieur's scary tales."

Collette sniffled and wiped a slimy trail from her nose onto my apron and skirts. "I don't feel well, Marie. I'm hot."

I touched her forehead with my wrist. She was hot. Too hot. "Oh, no, Collette. You are very warm."

Mère was laughing with a customer, Guillaume, a local man who too often left his wife and children to drink wine at our inn and make eyes at Mère. I caught her attention and beckoned her over, yet she refused to come. With a huff and stamp of my foot, I left little Collette standing by the kitchen door and went over to Mère.

"What is it, Marie?" She laughed, her arm slung easily around Guillaume's shoulders. I didn't like it when she did such things. Papa looked hurt, but the one time I'd seen him scold her, Mère had laughed and told him it was good for business.

"Collette is sick. A fever," I said, having trouble keeping the worry from my voice. I could not lose Pierre *and* Collette.

I expected Mère to drop her arm and go to Collette, but she did not. Her arm stayed where it was—wrapped around the fat, cup-shot Guillaume. "Then put her to bed and tend to her ills," she snapped at me, as if I were a meaningless, annoying gnat.

"But, Mère, she needs *you*." My eyes widened with indignation. "Will you not care for your own daughter?"

"That is why I have you." Mère took a drink from Guillaume's tankard. "Besides, I hear you spouted off at the market today, telling that fine young man you wanted to hunt wolves with the men." Mère and Guillaume snorted with laughter. "Really, Marie? A girl in the woods at night? Out to hunt a beast?"

My eyes welled with tears of humiliation, and she took another drink. "You try my patience, girl. If you cry, you cannot think. So stop your crying and play the part you so desperately wanted to play. Now is your chance to be all grown up, *mon chou*." Her voice twisted with spite. "Go outside. Gather herbs. You care for your sister!"

Guillaume whispered something to Mère, and they both laughed again. Ugh. Mère was drunk; she was useless like this except to sell more drink. Yet I couldn't forgive her for trying to embarrass me as if I were some foolish little girl—especially in front of the patrons. At least Tristan and Charles had gone home. I would have been even more furious with Mère had they been here to witness her verbal lashing.

I sighed. Fine. I was old enough to care for Collette. I would show Mère just what I could do; I didn't need her help or her cruel tangle of words.

Returning to Collette, I put an arm around her and hugged her close with the love I so longed to have from Mère, but knew I would never get. "I will put you to bed, then get some elderberries for you."

She clutched my leg tightly, her nails clawing at the skin beneath my chemise. "But not from the woods, Marie! You heard Monsieur Couture's warning. Not in the woods. Alone. At night. I do not want you to be lost like Pierre." A tear slid down her cheek.

I hugged her more closely, pretending my heart wasn't hammering in my chest faster than it should. I was seventeen and a young woman. I should not be afraid of such things. But what had I seen out there this night? 'Twas it man or beast or the treacherous imaginings of my mind?

"Oh, *mon chou*. I will check the kitchen first. But if we are out of dried elderflower, I will get some elderberries for you."

"But, Marie—" Eyes wide with fright, her words were cut off by Papa's booming voice: "The sun has long since set. You best get home or the wolf will eat you up!" Raucous laughter erupted from the local men, who had finished their wine and ale. "And if any of you has need of a place to stay for the night," Papa continued, "we can offer a room and pottage for just one *livre* apiece."

At that, two men I had never seen before strode over to Papa to ask after rooms and pottage. It looked like my chores weren't yet done for the day. I would now need to prepare the rooms and food, and then I would get Collette some elderberries to break her fever.

The moon was high in the night sky by the time I'd made up the pallets for the travelers and prepared the two bowls of pottage and wine. I was weary from a long day, but Collette seemed even warmer. Mère was busy preparing food for the morning, and Papa had gone to tend to the travelers' horses. I would not bother them with Collette, but would see to her myself and prove to them exactly what I was capable of.

I dug into the small store of dried herbs we kept for

fever and coughs. We had our winter store set aside, a portion I would not touch until the frost came. There would be no chance of restocking then, not with the ground frozen. Entire families died without their winter stores. Only crumbly bits of dried stems remained in my pot of elderflower from the autumn portion; not enough to treat Collette. I gave a deep sigh. I would have to go into the woods to look for more. I hoped that the weather hadn't turned too cold to find a stray elderberry still clinging to life in the moist areas beneath the trees. If I found none, I would do my best to make a tea with the dried scraps we had left—but I knew that wouldn't be enough for her fever.

With the words from Monsieur Couture haunting me, I steeled myself to return to the woods. *No. Peuh!* I told myself. *You are not going deep into the woods as you did when you followed the men. You are going to the edge of the woods just off the path to find wild elderberry bushes. Collette needs you to do this. And nothing ever happens at the edge of the woods.*

After tucking Collette into our bed, I pulled my scarlet cape snuggly around my shoulders and went into the yard. The chickens blindly clucked at me as I passed their coop. "Shhh. Hush, girls. Sleep. I'll tend to you in the morning," I cooed at them. I loved to get up in the morning and tend the chickens. I'd collect the day's eggs and feed them scraps from the previous day's cooking.

"Crazy birds," I murmured to myself with a smile, happy we had the benefit of so many eggs to fill our bellies. Mère thought they were dirty birds, which they were. But Papa and I thought they were funny. Pierre and I used to have such fun catching crickets and bugs, and watching the chickens cluck in delight as they gobbled them up.

I crossed the fenced-in yard that lay between our inn-home and the stable that housed Symonne and our few sheep. Beyond this fenced area lay our small garden, which butted up against the inn, convenient to the kitchen. And beyond the garden was a patch of woods with a path that led to a road, which led to the heart of Paris. I'd only been to Paris a handful of times. After I turned seventeen, Papa had allowed me to go along with him for shopping, and now that Pierre was gone, I was to go with him each month.

I reached the gate of the yard and stopped. Through the rustling of tree branches, the soft hoot of an owl echoed through the night; he was likely on the hunt for his evening meal of mouse or shrew. I shivered as a cool tendril of wind wrapped itself around me, and then I opened the gate to the woods.

The sooner I found the elderberries, the sooner Collette would begin to heal—and the sooner I would be in my warm bed, snug and safe for the night. Away from whatever man or beast might be lurking out here. I shivered, then took a deep breath of crisp air, and pulled the gate shut behind me, making sure the latch was secure. It would never do if the chickens got out—or a fox got in!

I passed alongside the inn, one of the guest rooms still alight with the tallow candle I'd afforded our guest. He coughed twice, then the room went dark. I continued past the house and along the edge of the garden, praying that some of the elderberry bushes I had planted there last spring would still have berries. I had harvested what I could in September before the days turned cooler, but mayhap some had escaped my eye.

In the pale light of the full moon, I knelt at the far western edge of the garden, searching for a sprig of elderberries I had missed. But none were to be found. I sighed. Collette needed the medicine. I supposed if I only walked a bit into the woods, just off the path so I could clearly see my way back home, that I would be safe.

Yes. That should be fine, I decided. I would get Collette some berries to chew or flowers to make tea, and all would be well. I pattered across a grassy patch so as not to get my shoes muddy. Lord knew the inn was muddy enough as it was. The hay-covered floor was sticky and clotted with mud from men tramping inside after trudging along the road to us. And each morning after tending the chickens, I swept the dirty straw from the floors, and Pierre, before he'd gone missing, would bring in fresh hay for us to spread. Now Papa brought in the hay after I swept and spread it across the floor.

In but a moment I reached the edge of the woods, my fingers cold, my heart racing. I looked back to our house and saw the darkened window to the room I shared with Collette. The thought of her lying sick and fevered in bed urged me onward. I turned along the edge of the path and went into the woods to the spot I had seen a wild elderberry bush only last week. Mayhap there were a few berries left to pick, and we could use the remainder for winter remedies.

The massive oak and sycamore trees swayed overhead, rustling their crisp leaves and blocking the moon from view. I found the wild elderberry bush easily enough, but it was small, and I had to crouch in the dirt to check for decaying petals or any dried berries not yet taken by squirrels. The leaves looked black in the night, and the tiny branches poked my fingers as I searched for any sign of fruit or flower.

After covering about a third of the bush, my fingers grazed a bunch of partially shriveled orbs. Elderberries! I could have sung with delight. But a howl in the distance brought my heart to my throat instead of song. The howl echoed through the trees, and then another howl from farther away replied in answer.

Yanking back my hand, I jumped up, my eyes darting around the dark woods. Goose bumps coursed along my flesh. I drew my cape tightly around me and took several steps back to the path. Back to safety.

The full moon peeked out from behind a branch, illuminating my path home. I could just see our room from where I stood—a small dot of light against the dark sky. A light. It had been dark when I left. That must mean Collette had cried out and Mère had gone to tend to her.

Heart pounding, I knew I could not go back to my sweet Collette, *mon chou*, without something to soothe her. And Mère was expecting me to bring tea or berries. No matter how much fear twisted in my heart, I had to go back and fetch what I'd come for. For Collette.

The howls had been in the distance, I told myself. Neither was so close I should be concerned. Still, I did not like the thought of being alone in the woods at night with wolves. Especially with no men or weapons nearby. Monsieur Couture's tale came back to me, whispering like a ghost in my ear.

Oh, silly girl! I shook myself, trying to clear my thoughts. It was but a story told to scare children and entertain their parents. Collette is warm and alive and needs your help. I chided myself for being afraid and turned back to the woods, retracing my steps to the elderberry bush.

I soon found the odd patch of dried elderberries again. My cold fingers fumbled with the branch, working to break it free, when something crackled in the woods. It sounded like a branch breaking under footfall. I stopped and listened. It couldn't be a wolf. Not so close. No. It must be a deer or some other animal that foraged at night. Quick as I could, I grabbed the branch and snapped it in my hand, stuffing the berries into my apron pocket.

In one motion, I stood and turned. Then froze.

Right before me, outlined by the full moon, was a wolf standing strangely on his two hind legs. His black eyes glistened at me, his teeth sharp and white. Before a scream escaped my lips, he pounced. And my world was shrouded in darkness.

CHAPTER 4

*S*traw filled my mouth, and my body was jerked and jostled from side to side. I forced open my tear-crusted eyes, but saw nothing save the faint outline of soiled hay and the side of a cart. My cheek brushed against something rough. A tight, nasty-tasting gag pressed hard into my teeth and cut into my cheeks. I could hardly move. Ropes bit into my wrists, trapping my hands behind my back, and my feet were bound. My head pounded with the sound of horse hooves clopping along a cobbled road, vibrating through my skull and bones. I tried to call out. I tried to scream. But only a whimper escaped my throat. We hit a bump, and the canvas covering me fluttered for a moment, allowing me a glimpse of the full moon. It was high now, but the sky was still black with night.

I tried to scream again, but the foul gag made me choke. I took gasps through my blocked nose. Struggling to breathe, I pushed and pulled and kicked against my bindings. Sweat seeped out of my skin, dampening my chemise, which clung to me in the chill night air. Still I struggled. Twisting and turning, my wrists and ankles burned as I strained against the ropes that held me. *Please! Papa. Mère.*

Charles. Someone! Please help me, I screamed in my mind, willing someone to hear me.

But no one did.

The only answer was the *clippity-clop* of the horse's hooves that carried me farther and farther away from Collette and home and safety.

Sweaty and exhausted, I sucked musty air in through my nostrils. *Calm down and think, Marie,* I told myself. *You must calm down and think.* My heart hammered against my ribs and into my throat, but I forced myself to lie still. To take long, deep breaths through my stuffy nose. If I could not keep my mind calm, I would not be able to escape. And I had to escape.

The cart turned down one lane, then another. People's voices, cup-shot and weary, echoed against walls and mingled with the *clippity-clop* of the hooves that stole me away. Soon the stench of urine and feces bit at my nose, and I knew we were in Paris. We had to be. I couldn't have been knocked senseless for very long. From my brief glimpse of the world, the moon was still high and the sky dark. I did not know where in Paris we were—just that people and buildings surrounded us by the way the horse's hooves and voices echoed. And there was the smell, too, of course.

Then I began to think of Collette and the herbs. Had Mère gone to the garden to get elderberries for her? Was Collette more ill with fever? Did they even know I was missing, or would they think I ran away like Pierre? Ran away because of Mère's cruel words to me? Mayhap they would not notice 'til morning. Tears leaked from my eyes upon thinking that I might not see Papa or my little sister again. So I began to pray.

Dear Lord, please let Mère take care of Collette as she cared for me when I was small. Please let Collette be well. Please, Lord, help her. Please be with Papa, ease his heart, and don't let him give up hope of finding me. And please, please help me escape from this . . . this . . .

I shivered as I thought of the howls I'd heard and the wolf-like form I had seen in the woods. Is that what had attacked me? Captured me? I had feared the wolves had taken Pierre, but not like this. I thought they had torn at his flesh or eaten him up. But could wolves drive carts? The strangeness of the thought gave me the desire to giggle and to scream. There had been many stories of werewolves in France. Some had even been captured and burned at the stake. But I could not have been taken by one. Mère and Papa said werewolves were not real. They said they were only made up to frighten children from straying too far from home. Stories like the one Monsieur Couture told to frighten and to entertain. They said those who burned as werewolves were heretics and nothing more.

But what if werewolves were real? What if one had captured me?

It was then I noticed something warm and sticky on my cheek, seeping into my gag—salty and metallic. I raised my head as much as my position would allow, but saw nothing but blackness. I leaned closer and sniffed. A metallic tang familiar from the spring slaughter of lambs filled my nose. Blood.

I jolted backward and hit my head against the back of the cart, sending a spike of pain through my already pounding skull. I tried to scream again, flailing to get free —even if freedom meant falling from the cart into the filth of the street.

Yet I was bound and secured, bales of hay keeping me prisoner. I tried not to taste the blood seeping in through my gag. I wondered if it was mine and shuddered to think of who it might belong to if it wasn't.

Suddenly the sound of the street turned into that of a deserted, dirt-packed alley. The echo of far-off human voices faded, and the cart slowed. Then I heard the cluck of chickens, and the cart stopped.

I felt someone dismount. The cart's wheels groaned, the departure of weight causing me to spring up a tad. A door somewhere nearby squeaked open, and a woman's voice broke the strange silence. "What have you done?" She made a strange, choked sound and hissed. "Not another one—so soon? You shall be caught!"

"Not if you will keep my secret, dear Marguerite." A thick, husky male voice answered her in little more than a whisper. "Now, quickly. Let's get her inside before the darkness fails us."

A moment later, the thin, scratchy barrier between me and my captor was torn back. I squinted up at him, but saw nothing more than his black silhouette against the moon. A brief shudder of relief rippled through me. I could not see him, but I could tell it was a man. A man in a cloak without a hat. 'Twas not a beast after all.

My relief lasted but a moment. He roughly grabbed me by my shoulders and tossed me over his back like I was nothing more than a sack of rye. The air whooshed from my lungs in a grunt, making my ribcage ache. Blood rushed to my head, and my eyes clouded with darkness. When they cleared, I saw nothing more than the brown hosiery on his legs and the dirt of the ground in the pale moonlight. "We'll have you settled soon, *ma chérie*. And then you and I can become acquainted."

I tried to scream in reply, but only a squeak came out. I twisted on my captor's shoulder, working to dig my knees into his back. His grip tightened painfully, and he carried me through a narrow door, its wooden frame scraping against my bare arms.

The door shut solidly behind us. *Keep your wits, Marie. Look and listen, just like Papa told you, and you will find a way out.* Though I was upside down on his back, I turned my cheek to look around. The main room, for I expected that was what we were now in, was dark and filled with tallow smoke. I began to cough, but choked on my gag. I tried to slow my breathing and remain calm, but I could not stop my heart from racing to a gallop as the man took me into another dark room. A few candles flickered, giving me enough light to see tables covered in cloth—wool and silk and taffeta. The beautiful patterns and colors seemed to shimmer even in the dim light. And there were tools. Sharp tools. I caught glimpses of massive shears and needles and knives. It looked to be a tailor's shop.

Before I could see anything further, my captor turned toward a small door. "The door, Marguerite."

I saw skirts and a woman's hand holding a skeleton key. She'd been so silent, I'd forgotten she was there. Without a word, she unlocked a solid wooden door and held it open. "Do not be long, Jacques. I still expect you for dinner."

Heat passed close by as she handed him a lit torch. He clutched me hard with his powerful right hand and held the torch high in his left. Then my captor grunted at her and stepped through the door, which was promptly closed and locked, plunging us into pungent blackness.

We moved down a narrow stairwell, my hips and elbows brushing stone walls with each step.

I saw nothing save darkness and an occasional flickering shadow born out of torchlight, yet my senses of hearing and smell seemed more keen. Along with his footsteps, I heard whimpering. Whether a dog or woman, I was unsure, except that it was high pitched and coming from a corner. Then there were the smells. They assaulted my nose and my senses. Dirt and blood, urine and smoke mingled with something else—something I hadn't quite smelled before. Something rotten and feral and fresh that I could only imagine was death itself.

My captor placed the torch in a sconce, then set me roughly against the wall, the cold stones hard against my spine. I tried to move, but could not—my legs and hands were still tied and growing raw.

The man—Jacques, I believe the woman had called him—turned to me. It surprised me to find him clean shaven. His face was normal, almost handsome, his eyes deep set. He took a knife from a table beyond him and held it before my face. "Welcome, *ma chérie*," he said without a trace of welcome in his words. "I will remove your gag, but if you scream, I will replace the gag—even more tightly. Do you understand?"

Eyes wide, I nodded. "Besides," he smiled, "we are deep beneath the ground, and no one will hear you scream."

I wanted to scream and spit in his face, but I needed to breathe and longed to have the nasty gag removed from my mouth. So I would abide his rules—for now.

He set to work. First, he cut the bindings from my ankles, then cut the gag from my face.

Once free, I took a breath, then spat into the dirt at his feet. I couldn't help myself.

He took a step back. "Don't get too fiery with me, girl, or you will regret it." The heaviness of his words and intensity of his eyes gave me pause. "I am to sup with my sister, then I will return so we can get acquainted." He tossed two pisspots at my feet. "Let your water go in one. Use the other for feces, but don't mix them," he said as ordinarily as if he were ordering a glass of ale at our inn.

Then he turned and left the gloomy chamber. I watched his back retreat up a long flight of stone steps. He gave three quick raps; I heard the jangle of keys and the bolt unlocking. Warm firelight flooded into the chilly cellar—if that is indeed where I was. After the door closed, it was once again damp darkness.

'Twas so cold and musty, I must be in the cellar or some other such storage room. Thankfully, he'd left the torch in its sconce, and as my eyes adjusted to the dim light, I looked around the room.

A large stone archway, yawning like a voracious mouth, opened into darkness on my left, the outlines of several oak barrels stacked neatly beside the entrance. Other barrels sat askew as if they would soon be used. Not far before me was a large table with what looked like fur and some sort of pale skins and leather.

The cellar's chill, damp air made me shiver, and I pulled my knees to my chest in an attempt to preserve my body's warmth. I went to pull my cloak around me, but found I had been stripped of it and my shoes. All I wore now was my chemise, my work dress, and my apron. Perhaps an escape would not be so easy.

I heard another whimpering moan. I looked to my right and saw a cage-like archway lined with bars. Inside I could make out what looked to be a heap of dirty rags. I stared hard for a moment, trying to discern what I was seeing—was there an animal nestled in those rags? A human?

"Hello?" I whispered, my voice trembling with my heart.

The heap of rags moved, scratching as if it had fleas, which it most certainly did. I hugged my knees more closely. "Hello?"

A nest of straw-like brown hair rose from the rags, and

a pale, gaunt face peered out at me. The eyes were sunken, flickering like hollow hell pits from their depths. It was not an animal, but a human who stared back at me. A young woman. Some poor wretch who had likely been taken like me and kept here for God knows how long.

Oh, God. Please save me.

Then she spoke, her voice like coarse rye being ground at the mill. "You will die down here," she rasped. "We will all die down here." Then she began to weep.

"Who will die down here? Who else is here?" I tried to look around, but the shadows were too deep.

Her weeping continued and tried my patience. "Listen, you wretched thing. If you cry, you cannot think. And if you cannot think, then we cannot get free. Now stop your crying and tell me what you know. Who is that man? What has he done to you?" I felt as though Mère were speaking through me, harsh and cruel, but I kept talking. I knew it was for her own good and for mine. Maybe that's what Mère had thought—that her barbed words were for my own good.

Eventually the sobbing slowed, then stopped, and the girl looked up at me again, her eyes wide with fright. She stared at me for a moment, then spoke in a horrified whisper. "Marie, what are you doing here?"

She knew my name. How did she know my name? I stared at her hard, and my blood froze in my veins. It was Nicole. Pierre's girl from down the lane.

CHAPTER 5

I awoke numb with cold, my aching wrist pressed against icy metal. I tried to turn over, glad to awaken from my nightmare. Glad I was in Le Poulet Fou on my own paillasse, safe beside Collette. What a wretched horror it would be to be captured by a beast! Yet as I turned, I found I could scarcely move. My feet were unbound, though my ankles throbbed where the binding had rubbed away my flesh. I attempted to rise, but found my wrists now chained to the wall by manacles. It had not been a nightmare. I was awake, and what I was living was real.

I clutched Nicole's hands through a gap between the iron bars that formed her prison. The memories of the previous night came flooding back in a wave of terror. Nicole was here. She and Pierre had not eloped, as I had hoped and prayed. She was here, and through her babbling tears, she'd spoken in hysterics of Pierre, but I did not understand much of what she'd said. Finally, she'd fallen asleep—exhausted by fear and pain. Somehow I, too, must have succumbed to my weariness.

Her dirty fingers still clung to mine, her head resting on

her frail, wasted arm. And there were wounds covering every patch of skin visible through her torn and filthy clothing. Some wounds were crusted with dried blood. Others were fresh. I tried not to cry, lest I should awaken Nicole. What had happened to her? What had this man—this beast—done to her? And what had happened to Pierre?

Before I had time to consider this or my circumstances, someone moved in the gloom and stood near one of the oak barrels. It was the man. The beast. He was here. In this room. With us.

He did not look at me, but was bent over his task. As I watched, he moved from a pile of dry white sticks over to the oak barrel and back again. Back and forth and back and forth he trod. He was so focused on his task, so purposeful in how he positioned the sticks, that I wondered what could be so important about filling a barrel with sticks. Yet I dared not utter a word, lest he turn his attention to me.

He filled the barrel to the brim before finally squeezing one last stick inside and pouring some liquid on it. Then, setting a circular lid atop the cask, he hammered it in place. When he was satisfied the barrel was sealed, he laid his tool on a table that was set back into a shadowy crevice I hadn't noticed without the light from a tallow candle he lit. From my vantage point on the floor, I could scarcely see what was upon it, save for the rough forms of metal tools. What would a tailor, if that's what he was, do with such tools in his cellar?

After setting down his hammer, he straightened his back and slowly turned toward me. His eyes met mine. They were dark and dangerous and full of desire. He held a white stick in his hand, tapping it against his open palm, and I feared he would beat me with it.

43

"Good morning, *ma chérie*. I trust you slept well." He took a long step closer to me. I clearly saw his pasty skin and clean-shaven face. His clothes were remarkably well made, which would suit a tailor. He wore hosiery of brown wool, fine breeches, and a creamy doublet of woven fabric. How could one so well presented be a beast?

He stood before me now, so close I could have reached out and touched him. Nicole awoke, stifling a cry, but the beast paid her no mind. His eyes bore into mine.

"Before we begin, *ma chérie*, I would like to tell you what I do down here." He tapped the white stick against his opposite palm again. *Thud, thud, thud.* "What I have done. What I will do to that weeping girl." He nodded toward Nicole, his eyes not leaving my face. "And, ultimately, what I will do to you." He smiled then. A cold, cruel, devilish smile. His eyes glinted evilly in the dim torchlight as he studied the stick in his hand. My stomach lurched, and vomit burned my throat. He held no stick in his hand, but a large, white bone. I prayed it was not human.

"First, I will feed you well. I shall stuff you like a pig being fattened for slaughter. It will be the most delicious food your lips and tongue have ever tasted. But that shall not last long. Once you are full and round and plump, I shall take the food away so your skin loosens on your bones." He licked his lips as he said the word *bones*, as if savoring a piece of crackling meat fresh from the fire and licking the drippings from his chin. "Then, when your skin is loose, I shall begin to remove it from you." He gently fingered a pale piece of leather on his workbench, and my heart jolted into my throat. It was not animal hide—it was skin! Human skin.

Oh, God. Oh, God. God, no. This could not be real. This beast could not be real. This terrible chamber of tortures could not be real. *God, please awaken me from this nightmare.*

"Help!" I screamed with all the force in my lungs. "Help! Help me!"

"Shhhhhh," Nicole spat, grabbing my arm through the bars, her eyes alight with fear. "No, Marie. You do not know what he'll do."

He stepped forward, looming above me. Nicole dropped my arm and scuttled away against the back wall of her squalid cell.

"You best listen to your friend, Marie." He said my name with venom, his dark eyes glaring down at me.

"Then I shall not eat your food or your drink!" I spat, fear and anger curdling my blood. If I could not scream, then I would fight. I would fight like Mère had taught me. Fight like she fought for everything she wanted in her life.

He tilted his head back and laughed—a laugh so cold and hollow it didn't sound human. He walked to his table and carefully selected a knife; he lifted it before his face, studying its iron blade. He held the knife up to the unclothed dress form and demonstrated as he spoke. "Oh, you will eat, *ma chérie*. You will eat what I give you, or you will cause immeasurable pain to your friend there." He pointed the knife at Nicole. "It will be up to you how she dies . . ." He ran the knife along the body of the dress form, beneath its slight breasts, slicing down the abdomen. "Slowly and with great pain." He smiled, moving the knife lower and thrusting it into the mannequin's groin. Then he yanked the knife out and sliced it across the mannequin's neck in a quick, fluid motion. "Or fast and with little pain." His voice rang as if a murmur, cutting my ears.

A heart-wrenching scream tore from my lips.

He grabbed me by the collar, ripping my now dirty chemise. "Do not scream, *ma chérie*. I do not wish to hear it," he hissed, then shrugged. "No one will hear you down here. None except the other residents, and they will not

45

help you." He arranged my torn chemise upon my shoulder, then stood back, studying me. "Then," he began again, in a calm, almost scientific voice, as if he had not been angry only moments before, "after I remove your skin and your screams have died away, it will be then that I will remove your bones. Only when your heart has stopped beating will I get to your ribs. A pity, really. I would so like to hear your screams as I take your ribs."

I was immobile with fear. Terror surged through my veins, but I could not move, let alone run. No one would ever find me. Not Papa. Not Mère. Not Collette. No one would ever know the truth of my fate and Nicole's and Pierre's. In that moment, I knew—if I did nothing, I would die here.

I would not let her die. I would help Nicole and save us both. Whether by brawn or brain, I would fight. And for now, I must use my brain and seek a way out of this horrid place. There had to be some way out of this cellar. Some way to escape this monster. His sister—what was her name? My mind churned with such horror that I could not recall it. Perhaps she would help. Certainly she would not sit idly by while her brother robbed young women of their lives, would she?

Still calm, the man whom his sister had called Jacques —but I would call beast and monster and demon—set the knife back among his tools. He picked up a tray, which he placed before me. On it were slices of bacon, bread thick with berry preserves, and boiled eggs. It was richer than any breakfast I had ever seen. He loosened one of my wrists from its binding so I could partake, but I had no appetite for such fodder.

"Now eat, *ma chérie*. Break your fast and clean the plate. If you do not, your friend will pay the price."

The nearly inaudible crow of a rooster echoed from

somewhere in the distance, making me miss my chickens and my home. The beast rose to his monstrous height. "I must go. But we will begin when I return."

He left without another word. I stared at the food before me. I had never imagined such a feast to break my fast. Nor could I have imagined I would not have the desire to consume it.

Nicole sniffled and scooted back to me. "Is he gone?"

"For now." I nodded numbly. I picked up a boiled egg and offered it through the bars to Nicole. "Eat."

"I cannot!" she shrieked.

"He'll never know." I shoved the egg toward her, and it fell, toppling into the dirt of the floor.

"He will," she cried. "He always does." She scrambled to pick up the dirty egg and pushed it back into my hands through her prison bars.

"You must do as he says and eat it all. Do it, or we will both be punished." Her voice cracked with desperation. "Please, Marie. Eat."

This was not the Nicole I knew. My Nicole had been a spirited girl who would put Pierre in his place if he was overly bold. How could she be so utterly broken?

I took the egg from her, trying to wipe away the grit on the apron that was still tied around my waist. I took a bite. Sand crunched between my teeth, yet still I ate. I did not do it for the monster, but if it is what I must do to calm Nicole, then so be it. As I chewed and swallowed, her breathing grew calm and steady. Rocking back and forth, she stared at me through a curtain of filthy hair and watched me eat.

Next I ate the bread. 'Twas fresh and smothered in jam. It was something like Papa would have given to me as a treat on market day. Yet here, in this place, it was no treat at all. As I took my first bite of bread, a little gray mouse

47

scurried out from a crack in the stone wall and scampered across my toe. I bit back a squeal. I did not like mice or rats and had helped Mère many times stuff the holes in our walls with oleander leaves to thwart them. On occasion, we had trapped them. Yet something about this mouse stirred my heart; I could not bear to think of her trapped as I was. She was a frail little thing, scampering near my empty plate, sifting through the dirt and soiled hay by my feet. She was simply a starving creature seeking food for her family.

Mère would be horrified if I did not snuff out her life, but what did I care what Mère thought now? She was not here to see me, and I was in no mood to see another creature suffer. I pinched off a crumb of bread from my slice and dropped it before her. In an instant, she nibbled it up, gave a little squeak, and then scampered back into the hole from which she had come.

I smiled to myself. I may be trapped, but at least I could do a small kindness for one creature. Now I must look to helping Nicole. When I finally finished my bread and bacon, I turned to Nicole. "All done," I said with a consoling smile. "Now what must we do to escape from this place?"

"There is no escape," she whispered, her eyes falling from my face to the filthy floor of gray dirt.

"Then what of Pierre?" I asked. She'd said he'd been here, but now he was not. That much I had understood from her tearful ramblings of the previous night. "Certainly he will send help."

Nicole's eyes filled with tears, which soon streamed down her cheeks and into her filthy hair. She took several steadying breaths, but the tears did not stop. "No, Marie. No, *mon chou*. Pierre did not leave this place." Her eyes were fixed to something near the table. I looked upon it, and my heart stopped. She was staring at the skin before which the monster had stood; it was suspended and stretched upon a wooden frame by twine laced through holes around its edges. From where I sat, I saw the ragged eye and mouth holes where a face had been. The hair. Not blond or brown, but sandy. I started to scream. It could not be. It could not be, and yet I knew that it was. The pale, stretched skin was not only human skin.

It belonged to my brother. It was all that was left of Pierre.

CHAPTER 6

I vomited my breakfast onto the ground. My throat burned, and my mouth tasted of rancid bacon and vile bread. The terrible truth of what lay before me rippled beneath my skin and twisted into my heart like a knife. Repulsed, but driven by the love for my brother, I lurched forward. My arms outstretched, I reached for the skin. I needed to touch him. Hold him. My Pierre. Yet what had happened to the rest of him?

I was jerked backward by the chains that bound my arms, still inches from the frame that held the beast's diabolical treachery. "Pierre!" My voice cracked, tears streamed down my face, and I reached for him harder. "Oh, Pierre! *Mon frère!*"

"Marie. *Shhhhh,* Marie. Hush now, or he will come back." Nicole was clinging to the bars of her cell, her haunted eyes begging me to be quiet. Now she was the calm one and I the distraught, inconsolable creature.

Weeping, I clawed my way across the dirt floor to where she sat. Reaching through the bars, we held one another. My body shook with grief like I had never known.

I gasped for breath, clinging to Nicole as though she were the only thing keeping me tethered to life.

Finally, after what seemed an eternity, my tears slowed, and I calmed my stuttering breath. After wiping my dripping nose upon my dirty sleeve, I brushed back a bit of salt-crusted hair from my face. "How? When?" Sickness coiled up in my belly again, threatening to strike. Not even Mère would have been able to retain her icy composure to such a discovery. "When did it happen?"

"Only days ago, I think—he has not . . . he has not begun the tanning yet." Nicole kept her eyes, kind and sad, on mine, away from Pierre's skin.

The tanning? What measure of torture had my poor Pierre endured? And Nicole—forced to watch the life taken from her love. Forced to watch him murdered. It was too much. I cried out again, but shoved a fist into my mouth to stop myself. Crying was weakness, and I would not let this beast see me weak. Nor would I let poor Nicole see me without hope.

"When I came, Pierre was in here." She gestured to her dingy cell of dirt and straw and iron. "And there was one other. A wisp of a girl." She gave an involuntary shudder. "She was so frail she could scarcely move. A heap of skin and bones she was. It was not long before he took her . . . he took her out and began to cut." She shuddered again and spoke no more. As if the mere thought of what she'd seen would make her heart stop. Perhaps it would be better if it had.

"Did he suffer long?" A strange numbness was overtaking me, my pain and fear being beaten down, hidden beyond my grasp.

"No." She gave a quick shake of her head, strangely calm. "I did what the monster bade me to give him a quick death."

"He is a monster," I hissed through my teeth. "A wicked, evil monster! A beast! A demon!" If we had any hope of escape, I had to keep my wits. I must use my anger as kindling and not let my tears douse it. I would not think on Pierre. No. Not now. If I survived this, I would mourn Pierre once we were out of danger. "Nicole." I grabbed her hands in mine. "We must take action, *mon chou*. When does the beast come and go? How long do we have?"

Nicole released my hands and slumped back into her pile of rags on the ground. "There is no hope, Marie. We are below the earth. In his cellar. The door is locked, and only his sister keeps the key. And then, there is the werewolf."

"The werewolf?" Surely the wolf-like creature I thought I'd seen had been only an apparition of my imagination. Surely the men and boys had been chasing a phantom in the woods, and not a beast. Unless the beast was the demon tailor.

She nodded her head, but would speak no more of it.

"Nicole?" I pressed her to say more, but she kept her eyes stuck to the spot on the floor and would not look at me. "A werewolf?"

She bit her lip, curling it back with her teeth, making her skin the wax white of corpses. Tears flooded her eyes, and she crossed herself. "I did not believe it, Marie. I did not believe the stories of Monsieur Couture or the others. I did not believe such evil creatures existed, but thought of them only as frightening fairy tales meant to scare children —meant to scare us from leaving home."

"Yet you do believe it now?" A sickening sensation flickered in the pit of my stomach, driving back the numbness that had taken hold. "What did you see? You must tell me, Nicole."

"When the tailor—for that is what he is—when he has

had his pleasure, then the wolf will come to fetch us."

I shivered, but again pushed away my fear, trying to take on the calm logic of Mère. For all her faults, Mère had a sharp mind and knew how to keep her calm. "If it is a werewolf and not an evil man, then how do he and his sister survive the beast?"

"I don't know, Marie. Except the wolf came for the other girl and for Pierre . . ."

The desire to scream for help welled up in my throat, but I did not want the beast to come back down before I had fixed in my mind some way to evade the fiend. "There must be someone who can help us, Nicole. What if we scream and call for help? Surely someone will hear us and come. A neighbor. A passerby. Someone."

Nicole shook her head violently. "They will not. Pierre tried . . . But when he did—oh, Marie, when he did—the monster tailor came down and cut off the girl's ears while she was still alive!" Nicole began to weep and shake, the composure she'd awoken with fleeing from her features.

True, it was a terrible thing to think on—having one's body parts sawn away and enduring the agony of it—but thinking on it would do me no good. So I forced it from my mind and thought of Mère. I recalled one night at our inn when Papa was away and Pierre was still young. Collette was wrapped warmly around me, and we were jolted awake by a scream in the guestroom.

"Stay where you are," I told Collette as I scrambled from the bed, gathering my scarlet cloak and pulling it snuggly over my shift. I lit the single candle that sat at our bedside, then quietly crept from our tiny room.

Mère was already in the hallway, a shawl draped around her shoulders. She held a candle high in one hand, a carving knife in the other. "We'll not tolerate robbery or murder in this establishment, Monsieur Gerard." Her voice was calm and firm and full of steel. "You will gather your things at once." A man's voice complained, but someone else in the room must have kicked the villain because he made an *uff* sound and stumbled into the hall toward Mère. Instead of taking a step back as I would have done, Mère pointed the knife toward the man and marched him straight down the stairs, out of the inn, and into the night. There had been no arguing with her. Once she'd been crossed, there was no going back.

I'd later overheard her recount the tale to Papa. Her voice shook when she told him, more full of emotion than any other time I could recall. I'd always wondered if Mère had cried that night, but nonetheless, her strength and sternness amazed me.

Yes, I had to be calm and brave like Mère. She had taken the situation in hand, and we had all survived it. Instead of emotion, I must focus on the practicalities if we were to survive. "What of the woman, his sister?" I forced calmness into my voice, trying to soothe Nicole and myself. "Will she not help us?"

"She rarely comes down, and I do not know if she helps him or ignores his evil to save herself. Though I have heard her . . . chanting. Before—before they took the girl and Pierre from the cell. She came down the stairs. She was dressed in a strange-fitting garment. Leathery and rough. She did not glance in my direction, but went into the darkness beyond." Nicole nodded toward the cavernous mouth that led into a tunnel at the opposite end of the cellar. "That's where they're taken before the end."

"What's there?" I asked, straining to see into the blackness. Was it a tunnel? A way to escape? Papa had told me of a cellar in his boyhood home that had a tunnel leading away from his parents' tavern. They would use it to more easily store and transport wine, which came in handy when the Church was discouraging drunkenness. Mayhap this cellar had such a tunnel as well.

"Beautiful and terrible her singing is, yet I cannot understand a word of it. After it stops, there is silence. Then through the silence, the monster tailor brings them back—or what's left of them. He brings their skins . . ." Nicole swallowed, clutching her hands tightly in her lap.

"Their skins?" I felt as if my spirit would float out of my body, leaving only my flesh behind so I would not have to endure whatever this wicked man planned to do to me.

Her head bobbed ever so slightly. "He takes everything. The skin. The organs. The bones. He told me he puts them in jars and barrels and tans the skins. If we do not obey, he will begin cutting while we are still alive. Just like he took the girl's ears!" She buried her sunken face in her bony hands and wept. "Oh, Marie! I do not wish to die this way."

I thrust my arms through the cellar bars and took her hands in my own. "While there is still breath, there is still hope. Please do not cry, Nicole. We must stay calm and ready ourselves for his return."

———

I was fast asleep when the jangle of keys and the turn of the lock pricked at my ears and brought me instantly awake. I sat upright, blinking.

A seam of light spilled down the cellar stairs for a moment, then the door closed behind him. His leather-clad feet slapped upon the stone steps, then his shoes and legs appeared. 'Twas the beast. The demon. The tailor. That is what I would call him: the demon tailor. He was coming back to us, and I must be ready to act.

He carried a tray with food and a sack over his shoulder. He set down the sack and the tray, then fetched the still-burning torch from the wall. He lit other torches around the cellar and then several tallow candles upon a table. The room flickered with light and shadows. The table held a multitude of instruments: knives and needles, scissors and thread. In the corner, to my right, was a blackened fireplace with a large cauldron set before it. To my left, the flickering light illuminated Pierre's grotesque hide, stretched and pulled almost beyond recognition upon the frame.

Vomit rose again in my throat, and I looked away from Pierre. I would not look that direction again. Ever. Breathing deeply, I kept my eyes on the demon tailor. He placed the torch back in its sconce and brought a plate over to me. "It's time to eat." He roughly set a plate of boiled eggs and a bowl of what looked to be salted pork stew before me, then picked up my old plate and returned it to the tray.

I scowled at him, spittle forming in my mouth. I wanted to spit and yell and claw at him, but if I did, I would lose my chance to act, and Nicole might lose more than that.

"Eat, Marie," Nicole whispered, fright lacing her voice. "You must eat. You must do all he commands."

My stomach turned, but I steeled myself to do what I must. I took a bite of the steaming stew. The meat was not tough and leathery like the pork at home, but fresh. Fresh meat was rare at Le Poulet Fou. The demon tailor must be wealthy. I chewed and swallowed. Chewed and swallowed. The meat was good, but it scraped against my parched throat like a fleshing knife. "Cider?" I asked without thinking.

"In a moment, *ma chérie*." He pulled a trio of skeleton

keys from his breeches. As soon as she saw the keys, Nicole began to scream.

"Quiet, girl, or you shall regret your noise," he snapped and unlocked the door to her cell. She scuttled away like a shriveling spider, shivering in a corner of moldy bricks and soiled hay.

"Eat," he told me. "And do not vomit again. You need fodder to fill your gullet and to stretch your skin and make you supple."

My stomach turned. I placed the bowl upon the ground, as it was quite hot, then bit into the egg.

The demon tailor went into the cell, towering above the whimpering Nicole. "Please, *monsieur*. Please, do not hurt me." Tears streamed in rivulets, cutting clean paths down her dirt-stained face. "Please."

"Hush now, *ma chérie*," he cooed. "It will not be much longer." She whimpered at that, but the beast hushed her and held a tin cup of ale to her lips. What a strange vision. The large, powerful tailor—the beast—holding Nicole like a fragile doll, helping her drink. It seemed almost kind. Almost. "Drink now. Drink. We mustn't have your heart fail before it's time." A stream trickled down her chin, but she swallowed as best she could. When she finished, he scooped her into his arms and carried her like a helpless child from the cell. She was so thin. So frail. She had never been fat, but healthy and full featured. Now her skin hung from her bones, and traces of her ribs showed through the tears in her chemise.

He set her so close beside me I could smell the filth of feces and urine upon her. The stench was all around us, but the foul stink wafting from her was fresh. I wished I could have bathed her and given her clean garments.

My face must have betrayed my thoughts. "You'll soon get used to the smell, *ma chérie*. 'Tis all a part of what we do here." He turned to me and held a key to the manacles upon my wrists, then tilted his head toward Nicole. "Do nothing foolish, or she will pay the price."

Our chance was nearly upon us. *Keep calm, Marie. Keep calm and be brave like Mère*, I told myself.

"Do you hear me, girl?" His razor-sharp voice cut through my thoughts, forcing my eyes to his face.

"*Oui*," I nodded. Yes. Of course, I would play his game. For now.

First, he unlocked my right manacle. I tensed, ready to shove him down. His eyes locked on mine, keeping me still. Then he unlocked the left.

"Up," he barked and went to grab my shoulders.

'Twas up he wanted, then 'twas up I would be! I thrust out my arms, grabbed the too hot stew from the ground, and tossed it into his face.

He howled in rage and reeled backward. I shot to my feet, grabbed Nicole by the arm, and pulled her up. "Let's go, Nicole. Now. We must hurry."

"No, Marie, don't leave! I do not want to suffer for your disobedience!" She screamed, but too weak to fight, I dragged her to her feet and pulled her up the steep chamber stairs behind me. Her legs were so weak she could scarcely walk, and her arms trembled, one hand clinging to the wall for support. So I placed her arm around my shoulder and hauled her along like a sack of grain.

"Up, now!" I yelled, pulling her as I climbed. Each stone step was cold and slick beneath my bare feet. My heart raced faster than my feet would move, but soon we were at the top of the stairs. Facing the door that would lead to escape. I steadied my quaking hand and gave the same stolid knock I'd heard the beast give: three hard raps. I heard the jangle of keys. The turning of the key in the lock.

"No!" a hideous growl came from behind us. "Do not open the door, Marguerite!"

With little time to think, I threw myself against the wooden door before Marguerite could relock it. Pain shot through my shoulder and down my arm, but I didn't care. What was a bit of pain to be free of this monster? The door flew open, forcing the woman on the other side to stumble backward into a small dining chamber.

"Jacques!" she cried. "Help me! We will be ruined!" The woman struggled to her feet as I glanced about the room. Fire flickered in the hearth to my left, and beyond was a solid door. Straight ahead was a window, not shuttered for the night. And to my right was a narrow doorway.

I lurched to my right, aiming for the closest door. But Nicole tripped at the threshold and fell to the ground. "Leave me!" she wailed, kicking her filthy feet at me. "Leave me! There is no escape. There is no hope."

The woman had a candlestick in her hand and rushed toward me. There was no time to pause for Nicole. No time to plead with her to rise and run.

"I will come back," I called over my shoulder to Nicole and kept running.

I was in a strange chamber now. One with no exit. Ahead was a whitewashed wall. To my right a small twist of stairs.

I heard a thud and Nicole's moan. A pang of guilt for leaving her ran sour in my gut, but I could not go back for her now. I ran on. Up the stairs—my only escape—perhaps through a window and out onto a neighboring roof.

"You'll find no escape from me, *ma chérie*," boomed the monster, thudding up the stairs behind me.

Sweat dripped from my face and between my breasts; it

slicked my legs, causing my garments to twist and stick to my damp skin. I reached the top of the stairs. To my right was a wall, ahead a closed door, to my left an open doorway. I lurched through the doorway to my left and slammed the door closed. It was a bedchamber. Grabbing a small but heavy wooden table from the bedside, I pushed it in front of the door to block his way.

Bam! Bam! Bam!

The beast beat against the door with all his force. "*Ma chérie*," he called, false joy quavering in his voice. "You have nowhere to go. Come now, open the door, and mayhap I will make your way easier."

I rushed to the window and threw open the shutters to scream out to the world for help. Yet as soon as I opened the shutters, my heart sank. A thick greenish-yellow pane of glass filled the frame. Glass? Where had he found such wealth? Perhaps by stealing from those he took and killed. Turning back to the room, I searched for something with which to break the glass, hoping the crash would make him angry. 'Twas a small loss compared to what he had cost me and Nicole. Our Pierre.

A huge *thud* sounded against the door and jolted the table toward me. One dark eye peered in at me. "Open the door, *ma chérie*," the demon growled. "Open it now!" He shoved his hip against the door and the table lurched forward.

Grabbing a lantern, I turned back to the window, pulled back my arm, and prepared to throw it at the glass with all my strength. It was then his powerful hand wrapped tightly around my wrist and yanked me backward.

"Oh, *ma chérie*," he scolded. "You would break my fine window glass? And cause a fire?" He made a tutting sound and removed the lantern from my grasp. Without releasing me, he set the lantern carefully on the table, then pulled me to him.

I tried to pull away, but he held me firm, his face mere inches from mine. His lips were so close I could see the parched skin as he wet them with his foul tongue. He smelled faintly of rosemary and citrus and strongly of sweat and rage. Taking my small hands in one of his, he thrust my arms over my head and pinned me against the wall. A scream rose in my throat, but I dared not let it out for fear of what he might do.

"What shall we do, *ma chérie?* You free my girl. You damage my door. And then you threaten to break my window glass. What shall be your punishment?" He shook his head and made the tutting sound again. With his free hand, he unlaced the top of my kirtle so it fell away, leaving my shoulders bare.

In the space of a breath he flipped me round and threw me onto his bed. *Oh, God, no. Please do not let him take my virtue. Not here. Not now. Not ever. Please, God.* Silent tears slipped down my cheeks. Tears were weakness, but I could not stop them.

His body pressed against mine. Pinning me to the bed, he ran a salty finger across my lips, down my chin, and along my neck, stopping at the top of my breasts. His eyes flickered downward, then back to mine. "I would take you here," he growled, his lips brushing mine. My stomach curdled and I squirmed to be away from him, but he pushed himself hard against me so I was unable to move. "I would enjoy it . . . but that might displease my master."

"Jacques!" His sister's surprised squeal made us both jump. "What are you doing? You must not! Not until it is time." The beast shifted his weight upon me and begrudgingly grunted assent to his sister.

"I have brought some rope. Bind her." Marguerite

tossed the rope to the monster, which he caught with one hand; then he expertly tied my wrists before I could even think of escape. Next he slipped a ringlet of rope over my neck and pulled until it dug into my throat, making me gag.

"Give her to me," the woman snapped, taking the end of the rope that bound my neck like a leash.

"Choke her if she tries to run. Hard. But do not kill her." His voice was like thin ice, cold and deadly. "I'll make good use of her later." He rolled off the bed and left the room without another glance in my direction.

Marguerite pulled me to my feet. My head pounded dully as she led me back to my prison.

CHAPTER 7

a howl awoke me. Not a distant howl from the forest like I sometimes heard from the comfort of my paillasse at home with Collette, but a nearby howl. One so close it rattled my teeth and prickled up gooseflesh along my spine.

I sat up with a jolt, glad not to be chained to the wall, but frightened at seeing the iron bars that caged me.

Scretch. Scretch. Scretch. Scretch.

A scraping sound drew my eyes to the demon tailor working in the open chamber beyond my cell. Pierre's skin was no longer stretched upon the frame, but draped across the table. With a long double-handled blade, the tailor worked to remove the hair from my brother's skin and scalp. Back and forth and back and forth he dragged the blade.

Scretch. Scretch. Scretch. Scretch.

Hot, unbidden tears streamed from my eyes, but I bit my lip in silent agony. Finally, Nicole cried out, pulling my gaze away from my brother to her.

No longer caged in the cell, she had taken my place at the wall, chained beside where the monster worked.

Fiddling weakly with her manacles, Nicole whimpered, then whispered up prayers to God. I barely made out her words against the monstrous scraping of his knife. "O most merciful Lord, grant to me Thy grace, that it may be with me, and labor with me, and persevere with me even to the end." She gave a weeping gasp, her words mingling with her tears.

"Nicole," I hissed and crawled toward her.

She turned her pale face to look at me, but didn't draw near. "Why?" she cried. "Why did you try to escape? Why did you take me with you?"

"Of course I took you with me. I will not leave you here to rot in this filth. We must try to escape. We must!" I reached for her through the bars of my cell, the cold metal hard against my bare arms, but my fingers stopped before finding her skin.

Clutching herself tightly, she began rocking back and forth and shaking her head, making no move to reach for me. "No, Marie. You should not have done that."

"Nicole," I said, feeling the heat rise in my cheeks. "I will not sit here and allow this monster destroy us."

"You do not have a choice!" she spat at me with such vehemence I flinched away. "You have signed my death warrant, and a painful one it will be."

My stomach churned with sickness, and my ears rang in the silence that followed. What was she saying? Were the beast's threats of causing her more pain for my actions true? Could he be so vile and cruel? The air of the dank room pressed in upon me as if great stones were crushing my chest, forcing the air from my lungs.

I gasped for breath, then I noticed the demon. He was no longer scraping his knife against my brother's skin. Instead, he was watching us, an amused smile twisting his thin lips in pleasure. When he saw me look at him, he set down his knife. "She is right, *ma chérie*. I will make her pay your debt, and you will watch."

Nicole moaned, pulled her knees to her chest, and began rocking and mumbling. Again her words sounded like frantic prayers, but I could not tell for certain.

"There is one last thing I must do with this skin before we begin our work on her," the tailor said as though he was directing an apprentice. He ran his hand along my brother's now hairless skin, then walked to a pot at the end of the table. He stirred the soup-like mixture, scooped a bit up with a large ladle, and then dumped it back, letting it splatter into the pot. "We must first tan the skin so it does not spoil. And all we have need of is here."

He gave another stir to the pot, then ladled the pulverized mixture onto the skin. "Did you know, *ma chérie*, that an animal's brain provides enough oil to tan a hide?" He ladled on another helping of the soupy gray wash, then began to massage it into Pierre's skin. "His brain was soft and ripe. Young. Perfect to soften his hide for our use." He massaged the skin tenderly as he spoke, and a sickening scream escaped me.

"Oh, Pierre! No. No! You monster! You foul demon!" I raged at him, the desire to claw out his hair and gouge out his eyes making me shake and sweat. I grabbed the bars to my cell so hard that my hands ached. If only the bars were his bones. I would break them into bits and have vengeance for my brother.

The demon tailor just chuckled. "Yes, we'll make him nice and soft." He ladled more of the brain mixture onto the skin and worked his way across what had been my brother's back. "So very soft. So very, very soft."

I gagged on my own disgorgement, but swallowed the rancid fluid back down, fearful of what retribution the monster might dole out if I spilled his stew upon my gown.

SUSAN MCCAULEY

Yet I did not remove my eyes from the tailor or his evil work. What could make a man into such a beast? Or was he even a man at all?

Nicole wept but, frantically crossing herself, mumbled a prayer. "Hail Mary, full of grace, the Lord is with thee. Blessed art thou among women, and blessed is the fruit of thy womb, Jesus. Holy Mary, Mother of God, pray for us sinners, now and at the hour of our death. Amen!"

The monster worked until he had massaged the gray mixture over the entirety of Pierre's skin. Front and back. He then rolled it up and squeezed. Oily juices leaked from the skin, dripping into muddy pools on the earthen floor. He unrolled the skin, then pressed dry cloth upon it, before rolling it up again and placing it on a small rack against the far wall of the chamber. "Tomorrow," he said cheerfully, "we will put him back on the rack to stretch him further and make him softer still."

He turned to Nicole, clapped his hands together, and smiled. "Now it is your turn, *ma chérie*."

"No!" Nicole thrashed hysterically against her manacles, straining against her chains with the little strength she had left. "Help me! Oh, God, please help me!"

The demon removed his keys from his belt, selected a skeleton key, and unchained Nicole. She struggled in his arms, but it was no use. She was too frail. Too weak. He dragged her to the table upon which Pierre's skin had been scraped clean. I clung hard to the bars, desperate to peel them back and help her. Yet they held firm and solid beneath my sweaty grasp.

The tailor thumped her body down hard upon the table, leftover bits of Pierre's hair and flesh and brain sticking to her skin. Nicole sat up and screamed, but he forced her onto her back, strapping first her wrists to the table with leather straps, then her ankles. It was no ordinary table, but more like a torture table Papa had told me about seeing once on display at a fair when he was a young man. It was solid oak with leather straps to hold the wrists and ropes to hold the ankles. There was a large crank attached to the rope as well—to stretch the person laid out upon it. I shivered, and fresh tears sprung to my eyes.

Screaming, Nicole buckled at the waist, struggling to break free, but he bound her waist with a rope, pulling tightly so the rope bit into her flesh. She moaned in pain, but now lay still.

"Arrgh!" I screamed, shaking the bars to my cell in frustration. If only I could get out and free her. 'Twas how I felt when Collette lay sick and feverish in bed and not even herbs seemed to help. Yet there was nothing I could do except watch and call out meager comforts to her.

"Nicole," I said, tears sliding down my cheeks. "Remember how you and Collette and Pierre and I would walk by the river after church. How he would pick you wildflowers and sing to us all?" The monster ignored my ministering, but a faint smile flickered upon Nicole's face, and I knew she remembered.

"Collette's favorite was 'Man on the Moon,' was it not?" I smiled, then flinched at my own words, thinking of the moon that had shone so bright and full in the sky the night the monster took me. But Nicole did not seem to notice, for I saw her lips tremble with the words—too terrified to sing. So I would sing for her and, mayhap, bring her some measure of comfort.

> The man in the moon stands and strides;
> On his boatfork his burden he beareth.
> It is a great wonder that he down does not
>   slide;

For fear, lest he fall, he shuddereth and
veereth.
When the frost freezeth, much chill he
bides.
There's no one in the world who knows
when he sits,
Unless it be the hedge, what clothes he
weareth.

My voice broke off into silence. The demon no longer worked, but turned to stare at me, a curious, scornful look in his eyes. He was watching. Waiting. Enjoying the moment of our memories as it was dragged out into the dank quietness. I did my best to ignore him, to bring Nicole a moment's more peace. "And then Collette would giggle and say that the man in the moon was naked."

Nicole smiled, but 'twas wiped from her face the instant the monster spoke. "I'll have no more singing." His voice rumbled through the stone-walled chamber, a note of finality in his words so even I dared not argue. Then he turned and selected a wicked-looking knife with a curved blade from his workbench. He studied the blade in the flickering candlelight and tested the wicked tip with a finger.

Dirty rivers of tears made their way down Nicole's gaunt cheeks, and she turned her head toward me. There was terrified pleading in her eyes.

"Please!" I screamed at the demon tailor, our brief moment of respite gone. "Stop this! Let us go home to our families. To our lives. Let us go now and God may yet forgive you."

The demon held the tip of his finger upon the blade and pressed until a pearl of blood pooled on his finger and ran down his arm. "God is not my master, nor do I seek his forgiveness."

I opened my mouth to say more, but Nicole shook her head slightly as if to say, do not make it worse. Her voice was a mere whisper, but I made out the words she wished to speak. "Pray for me."

Like all good Catholics, I believed in God, fasted according to tradition, and attended Mass, but I had never thought myself a godly person. As one who lived and worked in an inn flirting with my patrons, how could I be? I asked for forgiveness and gave repentance, but would He hear my prayers without a priest? I did not want Him to think me some Protestant heretic.

"Please," Nicole moaned to me as the demon tailor turned his knife on her and ripped its tip up the front of what remained of her tattered chemise. She whimpered again, and the beast wiped the trail of tears from her cheek with a rough thumb.

I sank to my knees, the ground cold and hard against my bare skin. I would pray good Catholic prayers and hope that God would listen even without a priest at my side. I crossed myself and began to pray. "Lord, you are all powerful. You are God, you are Father. I beg you through the intercession and help of archangels Michael, Raphael, and Gabriel for deliverance of my sister who is enslaved by the evil one. Please," I begged, "all saints of heaven, come to our aid."

Nicole screamed a painful, piteous scream. I dared not open my eyes. Her agonized wails beat against my brain like a drum. I could not bring myself to watch the horrors he was inflicting on her. All I could hear were her screams along with what must have been the ripping of her flesh and breaking of her bones. It was not long before her screams faded to whimpering moans. Weaker and weaker they grew, but I dared not look upon her. I vomited onto the floor of my cell. My vision swam before my eyes. The room spun. My guts churned.

"Look at her," the demon commanded. "Look at her, or I will cause her unimaginable pain."

I kept my eyes to the ground, not wishing to look upon such cruelty. How could anything be any more painful than what he did now? Yet I dared not tempt him—for Nicole's sake.

Nicole howled in greater agony.

It appeared I had no choice. If I wanted to save her pain, I must obey him. Steadying myself against the wall of my cell, I forced myself to look at her. The monster held a white-hot poker to what remained of the bloodied toes on her left foot and pressed it deep and searing into her flesh.

Her wailing ceased abruptly. The villain removed the poker and placed it in a small fire pit I had not noticed before. He then wiped his forehead with a cloth, smearing her blood across his face. "She is not dead, but taking respite in her senselessness." He held her face in his hands, turning her head limply one way, then another before releasing it to slump to the side. "I have begun with the left foot," he spoke to me as he cleaned his hands. "You will watch as I remove the toes from her right. If you do not, I will cut off your eyelids and force you to watch while I break her knees and cut off her nose."

I gasped, my heart racing to a gallop, and words failed me.

"Do you understand me, *ma chérie*?" This villain was beyond all measure of wickedness. Beyond all measure of evil. It was as if he were a demon masquerading in a man's flesh.

"Do you understand me?" he spat, his eyes blazing as hot as the fire that crackled behind him.

"Yes," I murmured.

"I cannot hear you." He took a looming step toward me, and I swallowed the wail of hopelessness building in my throat.

"Yes." I spoke with a conviction I did not feel. Yet what else could I do? I must obey and bide my time, lest I end up like poor Nicole. Mayhap there was some way to lessen her pain even if I could not help her escape.

She gasped awake then and gave a pitiful cry. "Mère? Papa?" Her glazed eyes flickered, then focused on the demon tailor. When she saw him, she gave a shriek and began to struggle as if she had just recalled where she was; she strained against her bindings. "No! No! Help me, Lord! Help me!"

"It is time," the tailor said and picked up the bone cutter he'd used on her left foot. "Watch now, *ma chérie*, or you will both suffer more than you can imagine."

Grabbing the bars of my cage, I steeled myself to watch his villainous torture, lest the poor wretch be put through even more pain. Upon seeing the jagged tooth blade, Nicole began to scream. Hysterical, blood-churning screams.

Then the demon tailor began his gruesome work, and the sound of metal tearing flesh and biting bone began anew.

CHAPTER 8

*N*icole's screams did not last as long as they had when the villain mutilated her left foot. She lost her senses as he finished his work on her right, having cut the toes from their joints and searing the flesh with his iron bar, lest she bleed to death and escape his horrific plans for her.

The demon tailor unbuckled her straps, ankles first, and then her wrists. He draped her limp body upon his shoulder like a sack of grain, and instead of turning toward the cell where he'd kept her housed, he turned toward the gaping dark mouth of the cellar. I could not see through the dark gloom. Was it possible he had more rooms in which to hide his villainous deeds? Were there other rooms in which to hide his victims?

With Nicole over his right shoulder, the tailor took a torch from the wall in his left hand and trod into the darkness. Just beyond the light of his torch, I saw what appeared to be a tunnel. The light began to fail as the monster rose with the ground, then turned right into another chamber off the tunnel.

There was silence for many long minutes, during which I sat alone in the cold darkness, eating the now tepid stew the tailor had set before me. Again, I had been served fresh meat. It was so strange he would feed his captives as well as a noble would treat his guests. I supposed he really did hope to fatten me up, then starve me to loosen the skin from my bones. I shivered at the thought, my stomach souring. The only good thing was that it would take time. Precious time in which I could discover a way to escape.

I had barely finished my pottage when the screaming began anew. To what horrors Nicole had awoken, I did not know. Her voice was broken and raw. Pure agony. And the terror that awaited me lest I found a way to escape.

The creak of the upstairs door opening into the cellar tore my attention from Nicole's screams.

The rustle of a kirtle scraping against the wall drew my attention. It was the demon's sister taking sweeping steps down the narrow stairwell, her torch lighting the gloom of the cellar. I was on my feet in an instant, my hands clenching the iron bars that trapped me. This could be my chance. Mayhap she would yield to my pleas and take pity on me.

"Please, *mademoiselle.*" My voice rose until it broke. I tried to steady myself before I continued. It would do no good to sound like a madwoman. If I was calm and rational, mayhap I could appeal to some sense of decency she still had trapped inside. "Please, let me out before he comes back. Help me escape and we can both be free."

She stopped in midstride and turned toward me, her eyes glittering in the light of her torch. "Do you know what this place used to be? What he used to keep here before . . ." She gestured to the chains on the wall and the manacles and Pierre's skin. "Well, before this." She gave a little shrug, letting her nails scrape the stained brick wall. "He kept goats here. And pigs. You know they aren't allowed to be kept in the city due to the stink and noise and filth. But Jacques wanted to have fresh meat and skin for leather." She sighed, appearing for a moment to have utterly forgotten me. "Fresh meat. He always had to have it . . . then he—changed—and the master grew hungry for something else. Something more wild and fresh and full of sin."

I shivered at her words, knowing she meant humans.

Her eyes focused on mine once again. She took two paces toward me and peered at the empty plate and bowl at my feet. "You poor creature, have you not been fed?"

"Yes, but—"

"And has he not provided a bed?" She looked to the pile of filthy rags and stale paillasse meant to serve as a bed.

"He's insane and you know it!" I snapped in a rush to get my words out before she left, all thoughts of being calm sapped from my mind. "He tortures and kills—"

The sound of a man's voice, hollow and wicked, began to echo through the chamber. A slow chant sounded in what must have been Latin. It sounded much like the words the priests read at church, except heavy with dread and laced with venomous excitement.

"Shhhh," she hissed and lifted her torch threateningly close to my face so it scorched the bars and made me flinch away. "He serves our lord . . . and I—I must be steadfast and true. A true and faithful sister. A true and faithful servant or face their wrath."

"Certainly God is mightier than any lord he serves," I whispered fiercely back to her, silently pleading with my heart to stay steady.

She hesitated, her eyes never meeting mine. Her torch

quavered slightly in her trembling grip. "You know nothing of our lord." Her face was a torn mask of fear and pain as she gestured toward the tunnel of blackness with the flame. "You know nothing of my brother! He will not cease. I know he will not."

"Perhaps. But you can." I gazed at the small knot of skeleton keys secured at her waist and reached out for them until my arms pressed painfully against the bars of my cell. "You can help me. Please, let me out. He'll never have to know it was you. I will run away from here—away from this place. I shall never come back. Please, Marguerite, help me."

The woman's eyes widened that I should know her name, and she took a step back. She looked at me for the first time, then let out a small cry of surprise, and placed her free hand over her heart. "Julienne?" she whispered, shuffling back toward me, inspecting me closely. "My sweet Julienne?"

"No. My name is Marie." I reached through the bars and clung to her wrists. "Who is Julienne, Marguerite?"

She stepped away again and shook her head. "No. No. No. No." She rubbed her face with her hand as if trying to scrub away some awful memory. "Of course you are not Julienne." She lifted her face in the smoky light and closed her eyes. "Forgive me."

The man's chanting grew louder, but I tried to ignore its urgency. "Who is Julienne, Marguerite? That is your name, is it not? Marguerite? Please, would you not help your own mother or sister or daughter from such cruelty and madness?"

"Stop!" she spat, her eyes suddenly fierce. "Of course you are not Julienne. My sweet, sweet girl. She would never turn her own family over to the city police."

75

A thought overcame me then, and I knew the truth. "Julienne is your daughter."

She thrust the torch so close I felt the heat lick my skin. "Yes. She was my daughter. My sweet, beautiful girl. She would not turn in her uncle Jacques. No matter what he did. She honored our master and gave herself freely."

"He killed her, didn't he?" I asked, horror filling my heart, tears filling my eyes. "Your own daughter. His own niece."

She studied me for a moment, then her eyes pooled with tears and longing. "You wouldn't understand. You pathetic Christian. You could never understand." She drew herself up with a breath. "She gave herself so he could transform. So his body could become a vessel for our master." A lone tear streaked down her porcelain cheek. "But you would run and seek out the night watch and have them take us. You would have them burn us for worshiping our lord."

Her lord? Did she speak of Satan or some other unholy monster? "No, Marguerite!" My tongue nearly tripped over itself in the lie I prayed God would forgive. I had not even considered what I would do if I escaped—just that I must escape. I would seek out the *Chevalier du guet*, the night watch, or the police or whoever would listen to me and stop this madness. "I will not call the night watch. I will run to my family and never look back. Please, let me go home to my mère and papa. You've already taken my brother, their only son. Would you take their daughter too?"

Something flickered in her eyes—pity or understanding —I wasn't sure which. Yet it was there. A thread of human compassion. I prayed she would allow it to take hold of her heart despite the chanting that beat against the walls and into my bones.

She reached a hand through the bars so only a whisper of her fingertips stroked my face. "My daughter. She was the first Jacques sacrificed to our lord. You look so like her." Marguerite's eyes welled again with tears, but she did not weep. "He said it was an honor. To be the first. My daughter. She died with courage—despite the pain. Pain I would have done anything to stop had he not bound and gagged me, forcing me to watch."

She looked at me hard, some silent battle waging behind her eyes. Finally she stepped forward, her hand trembling as she removed the bunch of keys from her waist. She held them out, just beyond my reach. "If he catches you, there will be no other chance. I can afford to drop these only once, and you must not tell him I did so with intent to help you." She turned her right cheek toward the light so I could see the scar that ran from behind her ear to her jaw. "He did this to me when I tried to stop him from giving my sweet Julienne to our master the first time. No doubt I'll be punished for this as well."

The keys dangled from her fingers, and after a final moment of contemplation, she dropped them outside my cell. Before I could utter my thanks, an unearthly howl issued from the guts of the cellar. A howl that made my blood run cold and my bowels churn.

With a look of terror, the woman turned toward the tunnel through which the demon tailor had taken Nicole. "It is nearly time. Go quickly! And pray to your god that he does not catch you." She lifted her skirt with her free hand and scurried into the darkened passage toward the sounds of the beast.

I groped through the bars of my cell, scrabbling in the dirt, trying to reach the keys. I strained against the bars until my shoulder ached against the cold metal. My fingers almost reached them. They were so close. If only I could reach but a hand's width more.

A sob escaped my lips, and I growled in frustration. Why would she give me such a favor and then leave my freedom just out of my grasp? I sat back in a huff, my filthy and torn chemise crumpled beneath my legs.

There must be something I could do. Some way to reach them. My eyes frantically flittered around the cell, searching for something to aid in my escape. That's when I spotted it. A single bone in my dish, the meat chewed and torn until only the marrow was left, which I had not sucked from the fragment. I scooped it up, wet and sticky in my hand. Broth from the stew dribbling down my fingers, I reached hard through the bars, the bone a gruesome extension of my own hand. I inserted the skeletal remains into the loop that held the keys and drew them to me.

The chanting grew louder. And louder still. Marguerite's voice crescendoed, clearly joining in with her wretched brother.

I rummaged through the keys, my arm at an awkward angle as I tried each one in the lock of my cell door. My hands shook so violently that the keys rattled and danced like sickly marionettes at an autumn fair. Then, finally, one slipped into the lock and turned. The ancient iron door swung open with a creak into the musky gloom.

I held my breath, praying that they had not heard it over their chanting. If this was my chance, then I must take it. I shoved past the heavy door and ran, my feet beating against the dirt of the cellar, and then against the rough wood of the stairs. My world was a whirl of sweat and fear and darkness.

The door at the top of the cellar was unlocked. I shoved it open and dashed to my left through their dining room. I passed through the tailor's workshop and wrenched open the front door. A gust of wind and needling pelts of rain struck me in the face. Thunder boomed and lightning flashed in the pitch-black sky, illuminating a sliver of the city. I caught a glimpse of Notre Dame beyond the rooftops and heard the faint throbbing of the cathedral bells calling out the evening curfew. I was in Paris. Not too far from home, yet far enough that I would have to run through the darkened, stormy streets to find my freedom. So be it. Rain and mud and thieves were far safer than staying here. Even in Paris at night.

Yet what of the murderers? Papa had said Paris was full of them—especially in the dark when there were too few torches alight and not enough night watchmen to keep us safe. I could just as easily die in the filth of the streets as here.

And what of Nicole? Could she still be alive after enduring such torture? Or had the vile monster ended her life? Should I leave her here alone and face the possible terrors of the Paris streets? Imagined terrors were safer than the reality of those that faced me, and I took a step forward.

Lightning illuminated a swirling stream of mud that ran through the street before me. Would Pierre have left Nicole to her fate and run for help? Or would he have gone back to take her with him? I knew the answer in my heart, but I dared not listen. I could not stay. I could not go back for her. Yet if I left, she would surely die. And then her blood would not only be on the hands of the demon tailor and his sister, but also on mine. I would be no better than a murderer.

The echo of Nicole's faint scream sealed my fate. I must have left the cellar door open for I could hear her anguished cries—her wail tangled with a fearsome howl that reverberated up through the bones of the house and into its very heart. I knew I could not leave her. If not for myself, then for Pierre. I had to go back and save her.

Molten lead filled my heart, dripping into my feet, but I shut the door against the storm outside and turned to face the gale within. My every step was heavy, sodden with fear. I crept quietly back to the door leading to the cellar. A gust of wind howled against the wooden shutters, which were tightly closed. Only a trickle of rain seeped through the slats and dribbled onto the floor. I wondered if Mère and Papa had many villagers at the inn tonight. Perhaps the storm had come late enough that the unruly louts had already gone home. Poor Collette. She was terribly frightened of storms. She always hid beneath the covers and snuggled close to me when it thundered. Now she had no one save Mère's cold comfort. Without me she was alone.

I stopped with my hand on the cellar door. I thought to save Nicole, but what of Collette? If this truly was my only chance to escape and I did not make it out with my life, what would become of Collette? Would she be destined to take my place serving the scoundrels whose hands wandered to places they should not go? I shuddered to think such things for my *mon chou*, yet I knew I must go on. Nicole was someone's daughter, someone's sister. What if it were Collette down there with the beast? Would I leave her? No. I would not. I knew if I returned to the cellar, my course would be set for Nicole. There would be no turning back until I had her.

Another howl echoed through the house, worming its way deep into my bones, and Nicole's screams intensified into bursts of horrific wailing.

Collette was safe with Mère and Papa, even if it was not the life I hoped for her. If I did not go back, Nicole would have no life at all. And so, without another thought,

I forced my fear behind me and stepped through the door to the cellar.

Ever so slowly I trod down the narrow wooden stairs that led into the gloom. The smell of smoke and dirt and blood bit at my nose with each step, yet I steeled my raging heart to go onward. In what seemed like a mere moment, I was past my cell and facing the black tunnel through which the monster had taken Nicole. I glanced through the dim light and torch smoke, searching for something that might help me fight off the monster and his sister. For certainly she would attack me if he were present.

I stopped just before the gaping mouth of the tunnel, looking for a weapon. Amidst the dirt and blood and scraps of skin, I found his tools. There was a knife and other implements for scraping leather. A wicked-looking pair of shears, needle sharp. The hammer he'd used to nail the casks shut.

A knife could cut. The shears could clip. But the hammer could crush. And I would crush his skull if given a chance. Then we would be free. I grasped the hammer firmly, feeling its weight in my grip, and followed Nicole's screams.

The sound of chanting reached out and drew me deeper into the darkness. Closer and closer I crept, my body swallowed up by the black mouth of the tunnel. The sound intensified, and the air turned strangely cold, wrapping its icy claws around me. On my right, I came to a doorway chiseled into the earth. I stopped. The scene that unfolded before me was one of unconscionable horror.

Flames leapt up at the drizzly hole in the ceiling, lapping at the droplets of rain that splashed through and licking the roof with black scorch marks. The woman. Just her. No beast. The monster's sister, Marguerite, chanted, her back to me. I could just make out what lay before her.

Nicole. She was naked. Her body slick with blood, her flesh ripped and torn around her breasts and belly. Tears streamed down her face. She struggled weakly, but could not move. Her wrists and ankles were tied to large white posts. They were knobby at the ends, the joints bound together with leather twine. Then I noticed they were not posts after all. Nicole was tied to a great white altar made of bones.

CHAPTER 9

*M*y blood ran cold, and my head grew light. The world began to spin around me. Gulping down short, quick breaths, I took a step back. I'd made a mistake. A horrible, gut-churning mistake. I should not be here. I should not have stayed for Nicole, no matter how much I wanted to save her. I needed help: the night watch, the police, a passerby, anyone! My heart thundered into my throat, threatening to strangle me. My muscles screamed for me to run, but my eyes clung to Nicole's gaunt, stricken face. How could I run and abandon my brother's love? How would I feel if she abandoned me to such a fate?

Against my good senses, I forced myself into the dank chamber, tightening my clammy grip on the tailor's hammer. Firelight flickered, throwing snakelike shadows against the mossy walls as the monster's sister came into full view. Her back was to Nicole, her eyes affixed to the tongues of flames leaping up from the fire. Beside her was a second bone altar upon which lay the corpse of another woman. She wore nothing save the tattered remains of a shredded chemise, and her skin was a waxy bluish purple.

83

Another victim the demon tailor had yet to fillet. How many of us were in the guts of this hell? How many lives had he claimed?

Marguerite stood motionless. Only her mouth moved. "*Egredere Marchosias. Nulla servus. Veni ad nos!* Come to us!" They sounded like words from Mass, but dark and twisted. I could not fathom what she said or who she called. And where was the beast? Was he watching from some dark recess I could not see? My insides writhed, but I crept forward ever so quietly. I must free Nicole. I would not let her fall to the hands of such wickedness. Marguerite kept chanting, her eyes fixed and unseeing upon some vision away from us. Good. Let Satan or whatever evil they hoped to reach keep them busy while I helped Nicole escape.

In a few dusty steps, my fingers met with the bloodied ropes that bound Nicole's waist and ankles. I was loath to set the hammer down, but what choice did I have? I could not untie the tightly cinched knots one-handed. So I set the hammer at the edge of the bone altar, fighting to steady my shaking hands. It took a great effort of will to keep them focused upon the knots that claimed her.

Nicole rolled her head toward me, her weary eyes sparking with recognition. She murmured something, but her voice was coarse like dry autumn leaves, and I could not make out what she said.

"Hush now," I whispered, scrabbling to untie her bindings with trembling fingers. "In a moment, you shall be free, and we will leave this place."

She mumbled again more urgently, and I leaned in to listen, my fingers never stopping their tiresome work on the knots that bit into her skin. "I cannot untie these cursed knots," I whispered, panic rising in my chest. I knew I must not tarry, lest the demon come back and snatch me. The thought made me tremble more; mayhap he was truly a demon and not just a wicked tailor.

Nicole whispered fiercely so I finally understood her words. "You must kill me," she said, her eyes pleading.

My trembling hands fell still. Nicole, who had always been full of life and joy and laughter, would not beg for death. "Please," she gurgled. "Do it. Do it now. Before he returns."

"Have you lost your senses?" Had she not already been so weak, I would have struck her face to bring her back to me. "You will live, Nicole. We both will. We must."

"Please," she begged, fresh tears streaming from her eyes.

"No, I will not! While there is life, there is hope. And I will set you free." I resumed my frantic tugging at her bindings, but then she gasped and her eyes grew wide as she gazed up at something just beyond me.

As I turned to run, a hand came down on my shoulder with such force that my spine felt as though it would snap like a twig. Yellowing, claw-like nails dug through my ragged chemise and into the skin of my right shoulder. I turned left, trying to pull away from whatever held me, but was spun around to face my assailant. I bit back a scream.

The creature who'd captured me in the woods met my gaze with red, feral eyes. His face was covered in hair, and his fang-like teeth protruded from the top of his mouth and cut into his bottom lip, which was crimson with blood. He was dressed like the monks from the Abbey of Saint-Germain-des-Prés I had seen at the market in Les Halles. A black cowl covered the top of the creature's head, the robes obscuring the entirety of his body—except his hands. His hands were ill-formed and hairy. His nails more like an animal's claws.

I yanked myself backward, the flesh of my shoulder

ripping with my chemise. I cried out in agony, but the beast held me firm.

"You should not be here, *ma chérie*," he growled. Despite the deep, guttural sound of his words, I knew that voice. It was *his* voice. The monster. The demon tailor.

It couldn't be true. Mère and Papa had said it was not. And yet it was. Monsieur Couture's tales and stories were true. Men could be monsters, werewolves were real, and I was Le Petit Chaperon Rouge. Little Red Riding Hood trapped in my own gruesome tale. Yet without my red cape, mayhap I would survive when she did not.

His nails tore the skin from my shoulder up to my neck, his fingers closing around my throat. I choked. I tried to scream. With a hand, he hoisted me up, trapping me in the smoky, bone-filled chamber where Nicole lay bound. I tried to scream again, but only a gurgle escaped my lips. He kicked open a door behind me and thrust me inside, splinters from the wooden frame wedging them-selves into the bloody, torn skin of my arms and shoul-ders. He dropped me roughly onto a thin patch of dirty hay soiled with dung. A musky scent, similar to night soil and stronger than the reeking streets of Paris, clung to the air and wormed its way into my nostrils, making me gag.

The door slammed shut, leaving me in near blackness. Only a slim crease of light shone beneath the wooden door. I banged on the door with my fists and screamed, then fell back into a dirty heap upon the ground and cried. The chanting began again, led by the monster's sister.

What had I done? Why had I come back? She had left the keys, given me my chance to flee. My one chance to escape, and I had tossed it away like a twig into a hearth fire. I should have run into the rain and the mud and screamed for help. Such fancies I'd had of saving Nicole and honoring Pierre were mere empty shells of hope that now withered and died in my heart.

"No!" Nicole screamed. She moaned for a moment. I heard her strain against her bindings, and then she gave in to weeping.

I did not want to see what was happening to my brother's love, and yet I could not stop myself from gazing out into the smoke-filled chamber. I lay down, my face pressed against the straw-strewn, dun stone floor, and peered beneath the door. My heart tore at my ribcage, and my arms were gooseflesh, yet I could see nothing but heavy shadows dancing in the smoky room. Nicole cried out, and the beast moaned. I couldn't imagine what he must be doing to her. I didn't want to imagine it. I slid back into my filthy patch of hay, sucking in deep breaths and whispering prayers to the Lord for Nicole's deliverance.

Finally, silence fell. No more chanting. No more weeping. No more moaning. Only the silence of the room and the occasional crackling of the fire.

After a time, I'm not certain if it was minutes or hours, there came a great snapping sound. The beast moaned in anguish. I scooted back to my spot by the door and peered beneath. My eyes adjusted to the smoke and dim light, so at first I could make out only vague shapes. Slowly the room became clearer to me. The demon tailor appeared to be a hairy beast. He writhed on the floor, his limbs bent at unnatural angles, his face contorted in anguish.

"Arrrrghhh," he wailed, his head arched back, his spine twisting beyond that of what a human should be able to endure.

His sister rushed forward and knelt by his side, obscuring him from my view. I started at her presence. It'd been so silent; I hadn't known she was still there. She had stayed the entire time? Watching as the monster stole

Nicole's virtue? Watching as he'd tortured her? I shuddered, wondering why she had aided me, and my heart
plunged into my gut. Any feelings of pity or sorrow I'd felt
for her twisted into hatred. No woman worth pitying could
stand by and watch another human being, another
woman, be destroyed. Marguerite deserved to die, as did
her demon brother.

I took strength in my hatred. I let it seep into my skin
and bones and heart, filling me up until my fear was
drowned in it. I knew not what I must yet endure, but I
would try again to escape. I must. For if I did not, this
diabolical pair would continue their evil work upon the
innocents of Paris. Upon other girls like Nicole. Or even
Collette. My gut writhed, and my heart nearly broke at the
thought. *God, no. Please keep Collette safe.*

The monster writhed on the floor beside his sister,
drawing my eye back to the pair. He screamed as his bones
cracked. The claws withdrew until only fingernails upon
his hands remained. The hair too was gone—his naked
body smooth save for that which fit a man—and he was
not a very hairy one at that.

Marguerite helped him sit up. He clung to her for
support. "It—never—gets—easier." His breath came out
in ragged, husky puffs.

"I'm sorry, *mon loup*. I wish it did not pain you so."
Marguerite spoke softly and brushed his dark hair from his
eyes.

He cocked his head back and glared at her. "If that is
so, then why would you allow one of our sacrifices to
escape?"

"I—" She opened her mouth to protest, but the tailor
lunged forward, encircling her neck in his hands.

"Jacques, stop!" She choked out the words, her eyes
wide with surprise. "I did not—"

He looked at her for a long moment, as if weighing his next choice carefully, then slowly released her neck and moved away from her. "Do not lie to me, my sister. There is no other way she could have been freed from her cell except with the keys kept in your possession."

Marguerite began to weep. She did not weep for my captivity, nor for Nicole's fate, nor for any of the poor souls who'd lost their lives in this hellish pit. Yet she wept now. And why? For disappointing her brother? The rage in my belly grew hot, and I wished I could reach into that foul room and strangle her myself.

The demon tailor stood with his back to me and pulled on the black robe that had been discarded upon the floor. "If you ever betray me again. If you ever think to betray me——" He turned to look at her, gleaming fury burning bright in his eyes. "Then I will see that you are his next sacrifice. Sister or no." Marguerite gulped back a sob. "Now get out and let me finish my work for our master."

Trembling, Marguerite rose from the floor and, clutching her chest, rushed from the room.

The beast turned to Nicole. "Your friend has caused you yet more trouble, *ma chérie*. I would have given you release from this world, but her efforts to escape have only ensured you will receive more pain before I dispatch you."

Nicole moaned faintly, and my heart fell like a mill-stone. How much longer would she survive? She was bloodied and bruised, her body limp. She hadn't even managed a whimper at the demon's threat. I wanted to kick down the door between us and rush to her. I wanted to save her as Pierre would wish. Yet I knew it was folly. Nicole would die, and if I did not come up with a plan soon, so would I.

The demon tailor took up what looked to be a small scythe, its curved tip glinting wickedly in the firelight. He ran it lightly over Nicole's abdomen and up to her breasts, the blade tickling her skin, but left no new marks. Then he leaned close to whisper in her ear. "It will not be over soon, *ma chérie*." With his final word, Nicole let out a guttural scream, and I lunged away from the door, vomit erupting from my guts as I heard his butchery begin anew.

Wiping the curdled chunks from my parched lips with a dirty sleeve, I began to pray. I prayed for Nicole. I prayed for her deliverance and for mine.

I rocked back and forth. And back and forth. Tears streamed down my face; the blood from each pound of my heart throbbed in my ears. I lost sense of time and place. All that existed was prayer and the smell of blood and the beating of my heart.

I must have lost my senses, for when I came to, there was only silence. No more crying. No more screaming. No more chanting. Only the tang of blood and haunting smoke filled the air.

Then the sound of sawing began anew. *Crech. Crech. Crech. Crech.*

I pressed my face to the seam beneath the door and spied the beast hard at work. Not on me, and blessedly, not on Nicole, who had either lost her senses or fallen asleep. The demon sawed through the woman's corpse I had seen laid out before Marguerite. I watched in petrified terror. Is this what he had done to Pierre? Is this what he would do to Nicole? To me?

He toiled at his evil work until nothing was left upon the table except for the poor dead woman's waxy torso and head. The limbs he stacked in a small pile as if they were firewood, then he took up a small carving knife and returned to what remained of the body.

My throat burned, and I thought for certain I would again fall into the dark oblivion of senselessness, but I forced myself awake. I must know what he did to his victims. To see that of which he was capable was to have a glimpse into his mind. Then I could glean some information to help set me free. And if free, I would tell the police what I had learned.

The beast placed the woman's brain into a bucket, much like the one he'd used when tanning Pierre's skin. I blanched with realization. He would use the girl's brain to prepare her skin as if she were a deer. And her bones . . . I looked at the main altar upon which her body lay and at Nicole's altar. They must be human bones. The bones of his other victims. There were hundreds of bones there. How many others had he already tortured and killed? How many more would endure this fate if I did not stop him?

My tendons flexed, and my muscles screamed at me to run, but there was no place to go. I was weak and trapped. The monster disappeared for a few moments, leaving me to my musings, but he returned soon enough with two chamber pots: mine and Nicole's. I gagged back thin bile, knowing full well what he meant to do with them. He would tan this woman as he had my brother. But what would he do with the skin once it was prepared? Would he use it like animal leather?

As if in response to my silent question, he bellowed for his sister. "Marguerite. Marguerite!" When she did not come, he laid the skin carefully, delicately, as if it were a piece of fine silk, over a rack near the wall, then went in search of his missing sister.

I sat back from my gruesome view, leaned my head against the wall, and shut my eyes. Yet there was no peace in the darkness. Visions of Nicole writhing in pain. Visions of her being mutilated. Visions of the demon tailor dismembering the corpse filled my mind. Then I began to hear a *drip, drip, dripping* sound from beyond my door. I peered again beneath the door of my prison and looked about the smoky room, trying not to gaze upon the woman's mutilated torso. My eyes snagged on her skin—to the place where her neck had been. I saw the lines from where her arms and legs had once joined her body. That's when I noticed the source of the dripping.

A thin trickle of blood ran down to a low spot on her hanging skin, *drip, drip, dripping* onto the floor. Like a tiny river, her blood steadily made its way toward me. My body urged me to move back, but I held steady when I heard voices. The demon tailor and his sister were coming back.

"I must see how it will fit together with the prepared pieces." He stood Marguerite by the fire and held up a garment of tanned skin.

Lord protect me. To use the flesh and bones was frightful enough, but now I saw his intentions. He was using human skin to make some demonic dress.

"Well, take off your clothes and try it on." Marguerite stared at him but a moment before unlacing her bodice and letting her garments fall to a heap around her ankles.

The tailor seemed unaffected by his sister's nakedness, treating her as if she were a lifeless model in his shop. He helped her slide the sewn skins over her arms, then stepped behind her and began lacing up the back. Only a small patch in the skirt area was missing, so her knees were still bare. "It will soon be complete, and we can attempt to raise Marchosias."

Marchosias? What name was that? Did this beast worship Satan? Or some other diabolical being? The desire to run poured through my veins, and my heart pounded. I wanted to scream and cry and flee. Yet there was no place to run. No place to hide. There was nothing to do except sit, save my strength, and watch.

Pressing my eye back to the opening beneath the door,

I watched as the demon tailor held up what I thought must be Pierre's skin and positioned it to see how it would fit in the skirt. He gave a grunt of satisfaction. "There is much work to do, but you will make him a fine wife. A bride outfitted in the splendor of his sacrifices."

To marry some creature named Marchosias? Wife to some demon? Was the beastly tailor simply evil, or was he also mad? Mayhap Marguerite was too afraid to say no to her brother's hellish plans.

Marguerite dressed with haste after the skins were removed from her body and left the chamber without a word. I sat back in my filthy hovel, resting upon my foul patch of hay, and wondered how she must feel to be dressed in the skins of people. People she'd met and fed and touched. I shivered. She wasn't as beastly as her brother, but she too was a monster in her own way.

Scretccch.

Scretccch.

Scretccch.

A ripping sound startled me back to my crack beneath the door. The demon tailor was again hunched over his gruesome work. With a wicked instrument in hand, he sliced deeply into the muscles of the corpse, and I silently thanked God it was not Nicole. Much of the blood had already drained, clearly revealing his victim's pink internal flesh and flecks of yellow fat as he tore his way toward her organs. I'd seen pigs slaughtered before and had helped Papa prepare the meat. I knew when the beast pulled out her stomach and intestines, her liver and spleen. He cracked her ribs and removed her heart. One at a time he placed the organs and chunks of flesh into a heaping, bloody mound.

When her corpse was naught but an empty shell, he began to remove the bones. Rib by rib, he began filling a great wooden cask. Once full to the top with bones, he dumped the contents of our chamber pots upon them. If only I could vomit or scream or escape. This was too horrific to endure. Not only had poor Nicole endured the loss of Pierre and been tormented and tortured by the demon tailor, but this was what awaited her if I didn't set her free. I must set her free. I must!

As if remembering me for the first time or sensing I was watching, the monster turned his gaze toward the door beneath which I peered. "I do not dishonor the sacrifices, *ma chérie*. The piss bleaches the bones. It whitens them and makes them pure." Pure? *Peuh!* As if this monster could even begin to understand the meaning of such a word. He was naught but filthy and cruel and evil.

"Nothing is wasted from the sacrifices. Not the meat. Not the bone. Not the flesh. Not even the brain. All I need is here. Her death honors Marchosias."

"Marchosias?" My voice escaped my lips in a rattling scream. "You are a monster! Marchosias must be a monster as well!"

The demon tailor took a menacing step toward the wooden door. Toward the only thing that kept me from his blades. His mouth contorted in anger, but then he stopped midstride. His eyes remained icy, but he began to laugh, cold and merciless. "You know nothing, Christian girl. I do not see your god here to save you. Where is he?" He held his hands up high and looked around the room. "He has not answered your prayers. He has not come to stop me in my work." He stared hard at the space beneath the door, and I was certain he saw me peering out. I shuddered and moved back a hand's width. Was the demon tailor right? Had God truly abandoned me to this hell?

"What power does the Christian god have over me? None!" The demon tailor turned his hands to his altars of bones. "Marchosias is the great and mighty Marquis of Hell. He commands thirty legions of demons. I will be Satan's instrument to bring forth Marchosias and his army. Imagine it, *ma chérie*, thousands upon thousands of demons brought forth upon the earth. And I shall lead them all. I shall rule alongside Marchosias. I shall be immortal!"

CHAPTER 10

*T*he demon tailor was gone for what felt like a day and a night, but in my dirty hovel, I could not tell the true passage of time. Only the rumbling of my belly and the dryness of my throat told me for certain that it had been too long since I'd last supped.

I lay back in my filthy patch of hay now wide awake. My eyes searched the darkness, seeking some crease of light that might lead to my escape. There was none but the dim crack beneath the door. With a great heave and a grunt of frustration, I kicked my bare foot against the door that held me prisoner. Then kicked again. The wood was solid beneath my feet, but I didn't care. Mayhap if I kicked long enough, I would make a hole, creep out through the labyrinth of his underground chambers, and then crawl away into the safety of the night. Sweat dripped from my brow, and I continued to kick, all the energy in my body devoted to this one mindless task. Yet I was thankful to have something at which to aim my anger and desperation.

Kick. Kick. Kick.

A splinter wedged itself beneath my toenail sending torrents of pain through my foot, but still I kicked. All of my fear and pain and rage was directed at the door that held me captive. I expected nothing but exhaustion for my efforts, but gasped in surprise when, suddenly, I felt a piece of wood give way. I stopped immediately and, panting from effort, scrabbled to the place I'd felt the wood collapse. My heart leapt with joy. There was a hole! 'Twas smaller than my Collette's fist, but still a hole. A hole that filled my heart with hope.

I grabbed at the wood, trying to work another piece free, but the slap of leather-clad feet stopped me. The monster was returning. His booted feet slapping against the floor of the tunnel that led to his torture chamber. I grabbed a handful of hay and stuffed the hole with it, praying he would not notice the damage I'd caused—praying he would not discover my attempt to break free.

"There is no reason to move you from your hovel." His voice echoed through the chamber, deep and intense. "You deserve no better for the trouble you've caused. But I will not let you starve." A jangle of keys and he opened my door. He placed a mug of ale, a crust of bread, and a bowl of piping hot stew before me.

My belly would not give me pause. I shoveled the soft, fleshy bread into my mouth. Bite after bite I savored the warm center and hardy crust, my stomach eager for the stew. The monster stood above me, smiling down as I devoured the fodder.

"I'm glad to see you've not lost your appetite nor wasted my sacrifices." He watched me closely, waiting for me to take a bite of stew.

His sacrifices? I stopped chewing, the chunk of bread turning foul in my mouth. What sacrifices? His coin for a cow or mutton? I held the food in my mouth, weighing his words, not wanting to consider that he possibly meant more. I swallowed, but did not finish the crust in my hand.

Then he laughed. "I see you have the measure of it, *ma chérie*. I do not waste. Each sacrifice serves the next. Soon the next girl's flesh will be prepared and ready for eating, then the next. Now enjoy your stew." Still laughing, he closed the door and locked it solidly behind him.

The horror of his words sank into my mind and corrupted my soul. It couldn't be . . . Had he been serving me the flesh of his victims? Not beef or pork or poultry, but human flesh? Had he fed me my own flesh and blood? My own Pierre?

I tossed the bowl of stew at the door with a howl of pain and fury and disgust. My stomach turned rancid, and I retched its contents into the hay, tears burning my eyes as the vomit burned my throat. I scrubbed at my tongue, clawing to scrape the vile contents from my mouth. "No. No. No. No. No!" I shrieked. What creature could be so monstrous? So evil? I rocked back and forth and back and forth. "Oh, Pierre. *Mon Pierre*. I'm so sorry, *mon Pierre*."

Teeth clenched, I was ready to fight—even if it meant dying. I would fight the monster with every breath in my body if it meant I had a chance at stopping his heinous deeds. If it meant I had a chance at saving Nicole and any others from such demented torture.

He was out there. Chanting again. The same sonorous voice calling out in Latin. I picked out the one word I knew for certain: Marchosias. Again, he was calling for the demon. Creeping forward, I yanked the hay from the hole in the door and peered out at him. Nothing remained of the corpse. Not on the torture table, nor on the ground. Everything was scrubbed clean as if his monstrous acts had never occurred. Only the barrel of bones remained, but it was now sealed. As for Nicole, he had moved her to the altar where the corpse had lain. She would be his next sacrifice.

"Venite ad me, Marchosias, magno et forti Marchionis inferos! Audire me facies potestas lupum!"

Lupum. I knew that word as well from Monsieur Couture. *Lupum.* Wolf. Was he again asking to be transformed into that fiendish monster? No matter, I was helpless to stop it. What could I do? Mayhap I could break from my hiding place and run free, and this time I would have no one to stop for. No one to return to. My heart clenched with guilt and regret and self-pity. I had tried to save Nicole. I had tried to save myself. I had tried and failed. I sighed, my heart heavy with fear and sadness, but with the knowledge that I had little other choice: escape or die.

I waited for him to leave the chamber, but he did not. He sat trance-like, facing the altar of bones. Then, after a time, he began chanting and calling out strange Latin phrases to *Marchosias*.

With the monster preoccupied, I again ripped and tore at the rotten wood at the base of the door. Little by little I widened the hole to a point that I could fit my entire head through, but not shoulders. There was no turning back now. There would be no amount of hay stuffing that would hide what I'd done.

His chanting grew louder and more vigorous. I prayed he would not hear me if I kicked. Upon my bottom, I faced the door and began kicking the frayed edges of wood with all my strength. More splinters dug their way beneath my skin, but I ignored the pain and kicked and kicked—each kick in cadence with the rhythm of the beast's chanting. A large section ripped beneath my foot, and I scooted forward to clear it away with numb fingers. As I did, I glanced at the monster to see what he was about.

In that moment, he tore his boots and robe from his body, letting the garment fall to the floor in tatters. He moaned and writhed, his back rippling and twisting as bones pushed their way up and out, forming overly thick and muscular limbs; hair sprouted from his skin like wheat, contorting his features from man to beast.

I was transfixed in horror, but soon chided myself for losing focus. The transformation would not take long, yet I prayed it would be long enough to allow me to break through my barricade. I ripped off the fragments of wood and judged the hole to be large enough—if barely—for me to squeeze through. I must go now if ever I would, while the beast writhed and twisted upon the ground.

He was not two cart lengths away, but with his back to me, it was my best chance to flee. On my hands and knees, I lurched forward, pulling myself through the dirt and the hay. Halfway out of my hovel and into the torture chamber, the back of my chemise snagged upon a rough plank and held me trapped. I wanted to cry out in frustration, but held my tongue, lest the demon tailor turn his attention from the pain of his transformation and onto me.

I pressed myself more firmly into the hard, dirt-packed ground, hoping somehow I would disappear into the earth and escape his sight. Gravelly dirt filled my mouth, and I struggled to move forward on my belly like an eel slithering in the mire. My chemise ripped, and a large splinter lodged itself into my back. Tears filled my eyes, and I let out an involuntary wail, but bit the tip of my tongue and looked to where the monster lay—breathing heavily and almost completely transformed. This was my only chance. If I did not go now, he would be upon me. Ignoring the stabbing pain in my back, I pulled myself forward. The splinter dug itself deeper into my flesh like a dagger, then blessedly broke free from the door as I pulled myself clear of the hole.

The beast was silent now, his breathing heavy. His

great, hairy shoulders heaved up and down. His transformation complete. I had little time. With feet sore from kicking and splinters, and blood seeping down my back, I quietly edged to the doorway of the torture chamber, my eyes falling once more on Nicole. She was still lost to consciousness. I prayed she would hold on. Hold on, Nicole. Hold on. Just long enough for me to return with help. I issued up my prayer and backed out into the tunnel.

Cool air hit me in the face and embraced my sweaty body with the promise of sweet escape. I backed away from the chamber door until I was certain he would not see me, then I reached around and yanked out the large splinter that protruded from my back. A gush of wetness accompanied the pain of release. I dropped the fragment of wood to the floor, then I turned and ran.

I groped through the darkness of the tunnel that led me at a downward angle back into the cell where the demon tailor had originally kept me. A few torches lit the chamber, and a quick movement in the cell caught my eye. A young girl with blond hair and a fine dress clung to the bars, her tear-stained face and pleading eyes staring out at me.

Marguerite stood close to the cell, a bowl of stew in her hands to feed the new victim. Her eyes widened at the sight of me. Before she responded, I attacked. In a surge of rage, I picked up the large stick the demon tailor had used to scrub the hides of his human prey and rushed at Marguerite. I pounded the stick over her head. Once. Twice. Thrice. She was down on the ground, her eyes unseeing, blood seeping from her scalp. The stew spilled down her front. *I'm sorry, Pierre. So sorry!* I tossed the stick down and turned to the stairs.

"Help! Help me, please!" the girl screeched. "Don't leave me here. When she wakes, she will hurt me!"

I stumbled to a stop at the base of the stairs that led up and out of the demon tailor's house and did not look back. If I stayed for this girl as I had stayed for Nicole, I would end up back in my prison, and we would both suffer at the monster's hands. Yet if I ran, there was a chance I would find help and send them back to free her and Nicole. It was my only choice.

In haste, I turned to the girl. "I cannot stay, but I will send help back for you. I promise." I leapt onto the stairs and ran upward, her screams and wails of pleading haunting my every step.

"No! Don't leave me! Don't leave me here!" she wailed again and again.

I pushed my weak legs and pained feet as hard as they would travel. Leaving a trail of bloody footprints, I ran up the stairs, through the darkened living room, and into the tailor's workroom. I threw open the front door, and a gust of autumn wind twisted itself around me, tossing my hair and garments about. The filth of the street felt like heaven beneath my feet. I was out of his house and into the freedom of the night.

CHAPTER 11

I heard a great growl from the doorway behind me, and before I could turn to look, the weight of a huge, hairy beast toppled me to the ground. Pain seared into my flesh as his jaws clamped onto my shoulder. Was there no escaping this beast? I was so close to freedom; I'd tasted it in the air, yet here I lay, pinned to the muddy ground, bleeding and in pain mere feet from the prison he called home.

Jaws still penetrating my flesh, the great wolf dragged me backward through the dirt and muck of the street. "No!" I screamed with all the air in my lungs, hoping that some neighbor or night watchman would hear me despite the time of night. "Help me! Help—" My voice was cut off as his claws clutched my neck and strangled my scream. I struggled and kicked, but I was like a helpless babe in his grasp. Soon I was back inside his lair.

Face bloodied, eyes glaring at me, Marguerite closed and bolted the door behind us. "You will get no more pity from me, *ma chérie*," she spat, her words dripping with venom. "I was wrong. You are *nothing* like Julienne." Then she turned her back upon me and disappeared into another room, closing the door and leaving me alone with the beast.

His eyes shone red like some supernatural star that glowed overly bright in the night. His black hair stood on end, his wolfish ears alert. He stood on his hind legs like some bestial man and watched me silently—as if surveying his prey.

My shoulder throbbed with pain where his teeth had dug into my flesh. I looked right, then left, praying for some avenue of escape—but there was none to be found. A wicked-looking candlestick sat upon a table nearby. Mayhap I could use it as a weapon. If I could not escape, I would fight.

I offered up a silent prayer to God and prepared to lunge for the candlestick. In a blink, I lunged right. My fingers grazed the candlestick, but before I grasped it, the beast was upon me again. The last thing I remember was his beastly form pressing down on me and his claws wrapping around my throat—strangling the breath from my lungs—before I fell into blissful darkness.

I awoke to throbbing. My feet throbbed. My shoulder throbbed. My back where the splinter had pierced my flesh throbbed. And for some reason the front of my torso throbbed. Warm wetness covered my thighs and belly, and it took but a moment for me to realize my chemise was torn up to my waist. Forcing open my tear-encrusted eyes, I struggled to sit up and cover my legs, but found I was bound to the same terrible altar upon which Nicole had been mutilated. I let out a scream of fear and rage, straining against my bindings.

"Good. I'm glad you are awake." The demon tailor's

voice startled me. Dressed in brown robes with his back to me, he'd blended with the wall, and I hadn't realized he was there. No longer covered in fur, and his body no longer misshapen to look more wolf than man, he turned to gaze down upon Nicole, who whimpered at him. "Your friend has caused more than enough trouble for me, *ma chérie*. More than any other." His words were like ice and chilled me to the marrow of my bones. He held up a great pair of tailor shears, the rust-tinged blades gleaming in the smoky firelight. "For that, she will pay the price. And you will watch." He turned to me then, the shears angled toward me like a spear. "To attempt escape not once, but thrice." He smiled with a look mixed both with praise and contempt. "But you will not do so again, *ma chérie*. And my master will be pleased with such a . . . fiery sacrifice."

He walked to the end of the table and stood at my feet. "It is not yet time for the next ritual. I must wait until the moon is full once again. Yet I will not have you think you can play such games with me without consequence." He opened the great shears and sliced them so close I felt the breeze of each snip of air against my feet. "A little nip on each foot will be punishment enough, I think, *oui*?"

I screamed, struggling with all the strength left in my body as I realized what he meant to do. Fear surged through my chest and into my throat. Every fiber of my being wanted to escape or die. "Oh, God, please help me!" I wailed.

The demon tailor paused for a moment, the shears placed around the little toe of my left foot—prepared to cut. I felt the sharp, cool metal against my skin and the promise of pain. "Your god is not here, *ma chérie*. I have already told you. This is the lair of *Marchosias*." He smiled again as if preparing to cut a stem for a bouquet. "So innocent at the touch, but so violent on the cutting." And with that he clamped the shears closed upon my toe, and the most excruciating pain I have ever known shot up my leg and through my body like poison.

'Twas blinding, searing pain. Pain beyond all imagining ran from my feet and through my limbs like fire. I wailed. And struggled. Vomit forced its way from my mouth, and warm, slippery blood dripped from my foot. I turned my head to the side and spat, tears mingling with the hair and vomit on my face. I shut my eyes and prayed God would answer me. Prayed He would save me from this wretched pain. Prayed He would make it stop—the fear and pain and torture. Prayed He would send me home to Mère and Papa. If only He would send me home, then I would be happy with a life at the inn. I would be content to stay forever at Le Poulet Fou. I would care for our customers, bear children there, live out my whole blessed life at our inn with Charles. Sweet Charles. What a fool I'd been to ignore his loving kindness. How blind I'd been to the cruelty and pain in the world. For now that I'd lost it, nothing seemed sweeter to me than home. And it was to go home that I prayed to God.

But no answer came. Only more pain.

"The girl paid for your first attempt to escape. That toe was for your second. And this," he said, positioning the shears around the little toe of my right foot, "this is for the third and will ensure you do not go running off again." He gave a great snip to the toe on my right foot. I felt my bone give way. Screaming pain shot through my body once again, overwhelming all other senses.

I heard screams, but was barely aware they were my own. The world was a blur of smoke and tears and pain. Next, the demon tailor came toward my feet with a white-hot poker from the fire. "I'll not have you bleed to death, *ma chérie*. No, there is much left for us to do together before you leave this world." He pressed the poker to my throbbing toe, and in a swirl of pain, I was swallowed by the blissful darkness.

I awoke to a world of blackness—darker, it seemed, than where I had been before reviving—with only throbbing pain as my companion. My throbbing feet overwhelmed the pain in my back and shoulder, making the hay that poked like skeletal fingers into my hair and back nothing more than an annoying nuisance. A shuddering breath and the scent of soiled hay invaded my nostrils, letting me know I was still in the hovel beside the torture chamber.

My urine fouled the remains of my clothing and my patch of hay. I sat up, nauseated by pain, and worked to scrub the piss and blood from my thighs as best I could. I saw nothing of my condition, but once the sticky wetness was gone from my skin, I turned to the throbbing of my bitten shoulder. Very gently I peeled back my chemise from the bite wound. The material clung to my skin and tore away clots and bits of flesh, but I knew enough from Mère that I needed to keep the wounds clean. Once free from the filthy linen, I tore a less soiled piece from my skirt and pressed it to the bite to ease the bleeding. Then, with a great gulp, I turned to my toes—or what was left of them. Seared knobs of flesh were where my small toes used to be. Seared and painful, but not bleeding. Not that it mattered. I would not survive this hell; I knew that now. And it was hell. Hell on earth as the demon tailor intended. God had abandoned me, and all was truly lost.

I looked to the spot beneath the door that had been my window to the monster's world, but it was closed to me. I ran my fingers along the place where I had created the hole, but it was now patched; boards reinforced the door, preventing even the slimmest seam of light to seep beneath. I was as good as blind—trapped in a world of stench and darkness and pain. Tears leaked from my eyes, the will to stop them gone. All my hope gone. I had nothing left but God—even if He didn't listen. And so I prayed.

"Dear Lord," I began. My voice scraped against my parched throat as it was born into the musty air. "Please, hear me now. I have no priest for confession. No one to hear my prayers, but You. So, please. Please, I beg You to listen. If not for my sake, then for Nicole's." I closed my eyes and waited—silently praying to hear His preternatural voice of grace. But nothing came. No sound or voice, save the beating of my heart and the pounding in my throbbing wounds. I opened my eyes again. They ached in the darkness, my ears ringing in the silence.

"Please, God," I wailed. "Let us go home. Let me go to Mère and Papa and Collette. Home to Le Poulet Fou. Let us go home or die. But do not let us suffer at the hands of Satan's monster a moment longer, I beg of You!"

Tears streamed down my face. Nothing was left in my mind or soul except pain and hopelessness. I balled my hands into fists, shoving them into my tattered apron pockets—something I used to do when Mère had angered me. If only she were here to anger me now. I'd take a thousand arguments or stern words from Mère in place of this.

I dug my fists deeply into my tattered apron pocket, and something unexpected crunched beneath my knuckles. I opened my fingers and pulled out a crumbly stem with fragile dried berries still clinging to it. I sniffed. 'Twas the elderberry stem I'd picked for Collette the night I was stolen away by this monster. If he had caused Collette's death by my absence, by taking me away from her . . . I would— *Argh! Please, God, let Collette live! Let Nicole live! Let me live!* The thought of anything bad happening to Collette filled me with renewed fire. I kicked out at the wall in frustrated rage. Rage at not being there for my sister. Rage at losing Nicole and my brother. Rage at my own pain and helplessness.

That's when I heard a strange sound. One I could scarcely believe I'd hear in this filthy hole beneath the earth. I listened closely. There 'twas again—coming from the back of the hovel, opposite the door—away from the place I had focused my attention of escape. 'Twas a soft clucking sound. I scooted through the filthy hay to the back of the chamber where the stink of dung grew stronger. Not dung, but chicken droppings and feathers. I closed my eyes again and listened. It couldn't be, and yet it was. I heard it clearly now—the clucking of chickens just beyond the wall that held me. If there were chickens, that meant a coop, and a coop would lead to the outside world.

I shook myself. Mayhap I was dreaming. Mayhap dying. There were no chickens here. I was in some tunnel buried beneath the earth—too dank and dark and dirty for any animal to live. And yet I heard them clucking. And there was the odor. I pinched the wound in my shoulder just to be certain, and the sharp pain ensured me that I was truly awake.

A lost smile found its way to my lips as I thought on my wonderful, foolish chickens at Le Poulet Fou and home. Home. Perhaps God was answering my prayer after all.

I hurriedly dug the musty, soiled hay away from the back wall of my hovel. Using my fingernails, now caked with dirt and grime, I scrubbed away the filth along the planks of the wall where they met earth. That's when I noticed a small sliver of light I hadn't seen before. I had been too focused on my crease beneath the door to think of any other means of escape. And yet here it might be. Hardly daring to hope I'd been given another chance to escape, I pressed my face to the dirt to see beneath the warped and swollen wall. A pale sliver of evening sunlight and swirls of dust met my eyes. Shadows passed before me: the pecking of beaks and scratch of claws. There were chickens. Feathery, smelly, beautiful chickens!

I pressed against the wooden wall, soft and rotting beneath my fingers. I pressed hard, and a small piece gave way. It would take too long to pry it out, and I knew not when the monster would return for me. He was so enraged at my attempts at freedom that he may not wait for the next full moon to rob me of my life—or Nicole of hers. I did not know. Despite the pain I knew it would cause, I positioned myself with my bloodied feet to the wall, the bulk of filthy hay behind me, and began to kick. Each thump sent pain shooting through my feet and legs, but I paid it no mind. I mustn't. I must ignore the fiery agony and stay awake if I were to survive.

Within moments the rotten wood fell away beneath the hammering of my feet. Chickens clucked and scattered, running from my white limbs that intruded upon their home. I kicked until sunlight streamed into my dreary hovel, and once the opening was large enough, I turned around and poked my head through the hole. I wanted to laugh and cry at the sight of the dirty, stinky, silly birds that gazed at me, huddling in fright upon their perch. "I won't hurt you, girls. I promise," I crooned through tears of joy.

Through the slats in their coop came the dying rays of the day's late autumn light. I did not know how long I had been away from Mère and Papa and Collette, but I knew it was still autumn by the color of the light and the nip in the air. Amidst much clucking, I pulled myself into the coop, my arms and torso immediately covered in putrid chicken filth. The stench made my nose burn and eyes water. This coop had not been shoveled in some time, but there was nothing for it. It was my only way to be free.

Despite the fetid stench and moist droppings that clung to my skin and ruined clothes, I dragged myself through the chicken manure. My toes and arms and legs burned as feces and feathers covered my blistered wounds, but still I crawled forward. A roach scuttled past, scurrying toward some hiding place safe from the sharp beaks searching for a meal.

Weak from pain and lack of food, I pulled myself up. My legs wobbled, and fresh pain screamed its way up my feet and into my legs, making me sag against the coop's wooden wall. I tested my weight upon my feet, and sharp pain tore through me.

To escape, I must run. To run, I must stay on my feet. I must find a way to stay on my feet. I tested my weight upon my damaged toes, discovering that if I rolled my weight inward, away from my missing digits, the pain was still there but manageable. I took one step in this awkward manner, then another. Through wet, sticky chicken dung up to my ankles, I walked to the coop door and released the latch, silently praying that Mère would have the herbs necessary to stop any infection I might contract.

The coop led into a tiny yard and alleyway, which must come out somewhere behind the tailor's house and shop. The chickens clucked and stirred, but too afraid by my presence, they did not run for freedom as I made my way out of the coop. I shut the door solidly behind me. I couldn't risk the chickens running loose and alerting the monster and his sister that something was amiss. If I yet survived this, I would send help back for them too. My clucking saviors.

The light was growing dim, the sun already sunk

beyond the shops and homes. In the distance, the bells of Notre Dame rang out their haunting toll of the evening curfew—clanging deep and resonating in my bones. Darkness would come quickly. I prayed I would find help before nightfall when all Parisians fled indoors to the safety of their homes. Away from the thieves and murderers and beasts like the demon tailor.

Before any further dangers could befall me, I hobbled down the alley, away from the monster and his torture chamber. I had to be far enough away from his lair that he would not seek me out. And so with a whispered prayer, I fled into the heart of the city.

The usual bustle of daytime Paris had died to a murmur; she was not the lively, noisy city I knew. The singing and laughing and cursing of Parisians drifted through the windows of their homes as they prepared for the night. Yet most shops were closed, the people too afraid to be out past dark in the city. And with werewolves about, I knew none would open their doors to me past dark should I call or knock.

My toes had started to bleed again, but I kept a quick pace over the dirty and waste-filled streets. Seeing Paris at curfew was strange and frightening. There were no lights save for one gas lamp I saw in the distance, marking the entrance of what I took to be Holy Innocents' Cemetery. If that were so, then I must be near Les Halles. The memories of my fine day spent with Papa at the market in Les Halles brought new tears to my eyes. 'Twas the same day I'd been captured by the demon tailor. If only I could see Papa again. And Mère. And Collette. My sweet Collette. My *mon chou*. I hoped, prayed, she was alive and well. My heart lifted at the thought of seeing them all again. Of going home.

I must find help, and hurry, for the light was nearly

gone from the simmering gray sky, and my body was growing weaker from hunger and fatigue and loss of blood. The night watchmen should soon be out. I prayed I would meet one of them and not a thief in the night or something worse—the demon tailor hunting to recapture me. My heart sped up with terror at the thought, urging me on through the deserted, urine-filled lane. Finally, I turned onto a large city street and sagged with relief that there was still some bustle as shops closed up for the day.

There, not more than ten paces from me, was a man in a leather apron, pulling up a shoemaking sign, preparing to shut his doors for the night. Tears began to flow as freely as my blood, and I hobbled as fast as my damaged feet would take me to the gentle-looking shoemaker. He paled at the sight of me, but I reached out and clung to him as if he were my papa. I collapsed in his arms, my body shaking and trembling with sobs of relief. "Help me, *monsieur*. Please! There are other girls in danger. There is a monster. A demon tailor taking children from their homes and murdering them. Please, help me!"

Holding me in his arms, I heard his voice ring deep and true—calling into the growing dark for the night watchmen to come. That is the last thing I remember before giving in to my pain and exhaustion and sleep.

CHAPTER 12

I awoke in the shoemaker's home. I was still in my filth-covered chemise and tattered apron, but my legs and arms were clean, my feet bandaged, and my body wrapped in a clean blanket. Men's voices filled the room. I heard the shoemaker and two other voices I didn't recognize.

"*Mademoiselle*, are you awake?" 'Twas a soldier who looked down at me. His face was young, his eyes troubled but kind.

I started at his words and began to rise, but the kindly shoemaker settled me back on the pallet upon which I lay. "Rest. You must rest. I've called for a nearby healer—a friend—to tend to you."

"No!" I screamed, my voice frantic. "There are two girls still trapped. There could be more. I do not know!" How could I have fallen asleep while they remained in mortal danger? I'd thought only of myself and the relief of being saved. The anguish of guilt wracked my body, and I let out a sob. "He has a girl—Nicole. And another younger one. You—you must save them. Please." I grabbed the soldier's arm, imploring him to listen. Imploring him to act before it was too late. "You must save them both! Please go before he hurts the girl and kills Nicole. Please, you must find the tailor and arrest him. He and his sister, Marguerite, have taken boys and girls. They have tortured and killed and eaten them!"

The shoemaker's face paled. The soldier squeezed my hand, then pulled up a three-legged stool on which to sit beside me. "Calm yourself, *mademoiselle*, please. I don't know what has befallen you, but calm yourself and tell me. I must have all the facts, and then I can act upon that which you tell me."

At that I began to cry with renewed ferocity. Would he be so cruel as to make me relive what I had just endured? Must I repeat the crimes committed against Pierre and Nicole and the countless others who'd been sacrificed to Marchosias for the monster's altar of bones? "Papa and Mère." I wept as though I were a small child. "Please, get my papa and mère. They are at Le Poulet Fou," I gasped through tears. "'Tis an inn at the edge of the city."

"We will send for your family when 'tis light, *mademoi-selle*," said the soldier. He was very young, not much older than me, but assured. His very presence commanded authority. "You are safe." He again took up my hand firmly in his. "You are safe. Now, please, tell me what has befallen you."

And so, with great speed, I told the young soldier and the cobbler about how the monster had taken me. I told them of all of the horrors I had witnessed. The healer interrupted my sordid tale, but also hastened the telling by revealing my many wounds: back, shoulder, feet with missing toes.

The young soldier grew pale at the monstrous deeds I described and the wounds I had that proved them true, and he soon left to fetch a lieutenant. He said he would take other soldiers with him and go to the tailor's house I had described to see if they found such a girl locked in a downstairs chamber. He said I would be asked to tell my tale to his officer when the day grew light.

The healer gave me some herbal tincture that eased my pain and made my head grow light. Once he and the soldier were gone, the shoemaker fed me thin broth and ale, and after again assuring me of my safety, left me to rest.

The morning brought a bustle of activity. The young soldier returned and escorted me to the jail by way of horse and cart to save my damaged feet from further pain.

I entered the wooden fortress and stopped dead. Before me, both with red-rimmed eyes, were Mère and Papa. "Mère! Papa!" I cried out, reaching for them with sobbing desperation.

Before my legs gave way, they were there. Mère's arms wrapped protectively—lovingly—around me. Papa embraced us both. "You are safe. *C'est ma fille.* Safe. Oh, thank God, you are safe."

Mère wept. She was truly crying, warm tears cascading down her cheeks and onto my face. She held me close to her breast and stroked my matted hair. I could not remember the last time she had held me so. "Please forgive me, my dear girl." Mère brushed my dirty hair away from my face and looked into my eyes. "Forgive me for leaving you to tend to Collette. Forgive me for placing such burdens upon you. Forgive me—" She gasped back a sob.

"'Tis all right, Mère." I hugged her even tighter, burying my face against her. But I had to know about my little sister. *Mon chou.* "Collette?" I hardly dared to speak her sweet name—hope and dread intertwined itself in my belly. If they were both here, and she was not with them . . . "Is she . . . is she well?" My voice cracked, and I prayed I would not endure another loss. I would surely not survive if she were dead.

Papa held my face in his calloused hands. "She is well, Marie. The fever lasted but two nights."

"But where?" I began, my voice hitching with uncertainty and panic. "Is she safe?"

"*Oui.* She is safe. Charles is with her at the inn. As soon as we received word they found you, Mère and I had to come, and Charles offered to care for everything while we're here." Papa smiled down at me with love in his eyes. "Collette has been praying for your return each night. We all have. Charles has been to the inn every night, praying with us and awaiting your return as well. He told your mère and me about his intentions to marry you and help with the inn. You have our blessing, Marie, if that is what you desire."

"And if Pierre returns, we will bless his union with Nicole," Mère said with a weak smile, all bitter harshness gone from her face.

At the mention of Pierre, I started crying again. I would have to tell Papa and the lieutenant what had befallen my sweet brother and Nicole. I did not know if I could bear it. It would be better if they thought Pierre had disappeared to have a life with his lovely Nicole. But I knew I could not lie. God had saved me, and Pierre's memory must be honored. My family deserved to know his fate. Nicole's family would be overjoyed at her return, but I doubted she would ever be the same. The young girl in his dungeon had been saved. The monster would be punished.

A police lieutenant with a thick face and piercing, dark eyes soon took an interview with me. I told the lieutenant all the nightmarish events I had recounted to the soldier. I trudged through the hell I'd endured, knowing the only way to stop was to finish the tale. I looked at Papa and Mère only when I had to tell of what had befallen Pierre and Nicole. My voice was gentle then, and my eyes filled with tears as my parents wept for their dead son. Their only son.

Mère clung to Papa as I told my tale, but they said nothing, their faces as white as sheets of linen.

I heard myself talking, speaking of the horrors I had witnessed and endured, but it was as if a stranger were talking through me. It was as if I were outside myself—there, but not there. The lieutenant told me that the demon tailor's name was Jacques Albinet and that the police had entered his home and chambers. "We believe he has killed somewhere between ten and fifty children. We are still uncovering—the bones." The lieutenant's voice cracked as he spoke to me and Mère and Papa. "You are extremely lucky to be alive." He looked at me gravely with sad, tired eyes. I knew that. Yes, I was alive. But I would also never be the same.

"He and his sister are raving about being *lupum*. They claim to be the werewolves besieging our city. They will burn at the stake for what they've done. And he will suffer the *Damnatio Memoriae*," the lieutenant said, his fine moustache twitching with pleasure. "His memory damned for all eternity. His very life will be scrubbed clean from the record books. There will be no memory of him anywhere. For his crimes, he will be forgotten to all but the devil and himself."

"Forgotten to all but the devil and himself." The lieutenant's words echoed through my brain. *Forgotten to all but
the devil and me* was a truer statement, for I feared I would
never forget the monster, no matter how hard I tried.

The lieutenant had excused himself from the room,
leaving me in uncomfortable silence with Mère and Papa. I
dared not look at them. I'd witnessed torture, been
tortured, seen my brother's remains. Would they view me
as damaged? Unmarriageable? Would I be of any use to
them at the inn once I healed? It was a strange moment,
brief but eternal, as I watched their faces process all the
horror that happened, that it was finally over. Then Papa
dropped to his knees beside me, and I wept in his arms
while Mère stroked my hair.

"'Tis over, Marie. Done. You are safe, *ma petite fille*.
Safe. And Nicole is safe. She will go home to be with her
parents. She will heal. And you will come home, and we
will always keep you safe. I'm so sorry. So, so sorry for what
you have witnessed and endured. Your brother—" He
gasped, tears strangling his words. "Your brother would be
so proud of you . . ."

The lieutenant opened the door and led in a full-faced,
sweaty man dressed in a fine silk doublet of scarlet with
golden hose.

"This is the girl who saved my daughter's life?" He
strode into the room as if we were not a family huddled
together in tears, and Papa stood to give the man the
respect due his social rank. Yet the man took no notice of
Papa or Mère and took my trembling hands in his large,
sweaty ones.

"She is," the lieutenant told him.

"You saved the life of my only daughter. My Kather-
ine." He bowed to me on bent knee. "My wife and I are
forever in your debt."

Mère and Papa stirred nervously beside me. Unsure of what to say or do, I said nothing.

The merchant pulled a leather pouch that clinked with coin from his waist and settled it heavily in my hand. "This is a token to repay you for your bravery. My daughter has only begun to tell me of the horrors—" His voice broke. He cleared his throat and began again. "Thank the Lord you saved her from whatever torture that monster had in store." Tears leaked down his jowls and into his beard. "You have saved my little girl from God only knows what suffering." He closed my hand tightly around the bag. "This gold is to help you and your family." He glanced at Mère and Papa. "Yet it is not enough."

His gray eyes met mine; they swirled with pain and concern and relief. "I have three sons. My eldest is already wed, but I would offer you a match with one of the youngers. You would be well kept and have a home in Paris. I would ensure you have all that you desire."

I heard Mère gasp and Papa shuffle. It was beyond belief or my greatest imaginings. It was what I had always longed for—an escape from my life at Le Poulet Fou. I'd endured such horrors to be faced with such a reward. Here was a wealthy man, kneeling before me as if I were his queen and not an innkeeper's daughter, offering me every-thing I'd always wanted. Everything I'd always dreamed of. Yet in that moment, I knew there was nothing else I would rather be. I was an innkeeper's daughter. I had parents who loved me, despite their faults. A sister who needed me. A man who not only wanted to marry me, but who loved me. I had love and a bed and a home. I had had every-thing a young woman could desire but had wanted more. No longer. I no longer wanted more. My dreams had changed. *I* had changed. And now all I wanted was the promise of family and of being home.

"Thank you, *monsieur*," I heard myself say. "This will surely help my family and our inn," I said of the gold, which I handed to Mère for safekeeping. "And I thank you for your kind and generous offer to be wed to one of your sons, but I cannot take such a gift. Not after what has happened. For now, my greatest wish in all the world is to be home with my papa and mère. That is my life and where I want to be." I expected Mère to object, but she said nothing. She made not even the tiniest squeak of protest, but simply squeezed my hand, and I glanced up in time to see Papa smile.

"You are young, but wise." The merchant smiled at me and rose, speaking to us all. "If ever you or your family have need, you have only to send word to Claude du Corbier, and my family and I will be at your service."

It had been a week since my escape from the demon tailor, but all I had endured haunted me. After Monsieur Corbier left and the lieutenant completed my interview, the young soldier had returned and told me they had found what was left of the dead woman, her flesh still soaking in a mixture made of her brains. From what I understood, nothing was left of Pierre—at least nothing they could identify as my poor brother. All they found were the partially finished garment made of skin and the bones. Lots and lots of bones. Bones that made up the altar. Bones being bleached with urine in barrels. Bones and human meat being salted and prepared for food. I tried not to think on such things but instead worked as much as my still healing feet would allow and spent time reading to Collette.

Today, though, was a day I could not escape my thoughts of the demon tailor or his sister or what had befallen that poor woman or Nicole or Pierre. Today the beast would die. Nicole stayed home with her parents, for she was not well enough to travel, and they had no mind to leave her alone. So, in our stead, Mère and Papa had gone to join the lieutenant and the citizens of Paris to watch the monster and his sister burn alive at the stake.

I used to think such a death was too barbarous for any sin, but I did not believe that anymore. They deserved all the pain they got for what they did to Pierre and Nicole and those countless other souls they had murdered. Perhaps God would have mercy on their souls; I never would.

Mère had tried to persuade me to go with them, to help ease my nightmares and put to rest my torturous memories, but I had no desire to lay eyes on the demon tailor ever again—even if his name was going to be wiped from history as the lieutenant told me.

No, I stayed at home to nurse my toes, watch Collette, and help Charles with the inn. My sweet Charles, who brings the poultice for my toes and serves me lunch and gathers fresh herbs each day to ease my pain and sadness. Despite the deformities I received from the beast, Charles loves me still. Papa says his love is true. Mère says he will make a good living for us at the inn and will be a fine husband. Collette thinks he's funny. I think he's kind.

For Charles has accepted me. He loves me, despite my deepest, darkest secret. For I am with child, and 'tis not his. The thing that grows inside me was spawn from the demon who robbed me of my virtue when I was senseless to the world. I do not know if the child will be born a human or a werewolf, a sweet babe or a monster. Charles prays with me. He tells me that whatever comes, we will care for it together—or, together, bring about its death.

ACKNOWLEDGMENTS

First, thank you readers for giving this book life. Your support is truly appreciated. I wrote this for those of you who were hungering for something "darker" from me. While my passion is writing middle grade and young adult fiction, this story sank its teeth into me and wouldn't let go. While I tried to make it fit the young adult genre, the story simply demanded more than was appropriate for that age group. Regardless of category, I hope you enjoyed my work.

I must thank my amazing editor, Deborah Halverson, who has supported and encouraged me through my journey of writing. Thanks also to the amazing cover designer Christian Bentulan for his stunning cover work. Thank you to everyone who has helped me with publicity and marketing. And, last, but definitely not least, thank you to my fabulous attorney, Charlotte A. Hassett, Esq., for her sound legal counsel and for keeping me grounded when I'm overwhelmed.

Many thanks to Hélène Visentin, Associate Dean of the Faculty and Professor of French Studies at Smith College, who helped me find the map I needed in an attempt to get the layout of late 16th century Paris correct in my telling of this twisted tale. Thanks to Peter Adam Salomon for giving me guidance as I grappled with the darker content of this story. And thank you to Pat Cuchens, my sweet friend and grammar guru, who catches pretty much all of my typos and grammar snafus, and who lends her emotional support whenever I need it; to the fabulous T.J. Resler, who writes amazing *National Geographic* books for kids and makes writing conferences so much fun. Thank you to my friends at the Horror Writers Association (HWA) for supporting and encouraging me and so many writers. And thanks to all of my family and friends who have believed in me and my writing over the years.

Finally, thank you to my mother, Sandy Basso, who reads and gives me feedback on everything I write; I don't know what I would do without you. And, last, but certainly not least, thank you to my husband, Rick, and my son, Alex, who have supported me through the ups and downs of the writing process, have had patience when I had to write despite them wanting me to do something else, and for their endless love and support.

ABOUT THE AUTHOR

Susan McCauley has been intrigued by ghost stories since she was first enchanted and scared witless on Disney's Haunted Mansion ride at the age of three. She now writes works of horror, paranormal, and dark fantasy (with a particular fondness for ghost stories). She lives in Houston, Texas, with her husband, son, three crazy cats, and a wide variety of other pets.

To get the latest news, check out www.sbmccauley.com or connect with her on social media.

If you enjoyed this book, please leave a review with your favorite book retailer, on Goodreads, or both—it will be immensely appreciated!

ALSO BY SUSAN MCCAULEY

The Devil's Tree

Ghost Hunters: Bones in the Wall

Made in the USA
Monee, IL
09 September 2021

76862443R00080